# Some Thoughts on Sylvia Iparraguirre's *Tierra del Fuego*

by

## Matthew N. Proser

Curbstone Press

# SYLVIA IPARRAGUIRRE
## *TIERRA DEL FUEGO*

—Matthew N. Proser

Today, in the middle of this emptiness, something
extraordinary happened. So rarely does the plain break its
endless monotony that when the dot wavering on the horizon
grew until it turned into a rider, and when it was obvious that
these poor homes were his goal, our impatience — if watching
with a quiet eye stubbornly trained on the horizon can be so
called — already had us waiting for him. This was indeed
something unusual, and yet watching from my house,
separated from the others by a league as he came right toward
us, I couldn't even dream of its true importance.

Thus begins Sylvia Iparraguirre's remarkable new novel
in its English translation by Hardie St. Martin, a version which
the author herself characterizes as "a splendid translation, very
good work."* The setting is Argentina and London in the mid-
nineteenth century, and this very first paragraph exhibits some
of the book's signal characteristics: suspense, precise
observation and detail, the evocation of an older writing style
without a sense of imitation and constraint, and the ability to
plunge directly and economically into the state of mind of a
key character. The year is 1865. The speaker — or writer in
this case, since these words are in fact being written in a journal
— is a 53 year old "blond" gaucho and retired sailor, John
William Guevara, the son of an English sailor, William Scott
Mallory, and a native Argentine woman, Lucía de Guevara,
whom Mallory never married, and the dot on the horizon will
materialize into a rider bringing a life-defining letter from a

functionary of the British Admiralty in London. "Mr. MacDowell or MacDowness" (since the paper is folded exactly where the signature has been written) requests that Guevara recount the details of a journey he made years ago on a British ship-of-sail along with the novel's focal figure, "Jemmy Button," all the way to the Tierra del Fuego and Cape Horn, "the continent's southernmost islands, where oceans furiously converge."

What was the nature of this voyage and what is the significance of its events? In attempting to respond to the request, but then transforming the task into a journal clearly no longer meant for the eyes of MacDowell or MacDowness, "Jack" Guevara takes on the burden of opening out his life and experience, both past and present, on paper: a progress of words and events, and responses to events, that stretches from the pampas of Buenos Aires Province in the new world and the colonial cities of Buenos Aires and Montevideo to the Tierra del Fuego — home of the Yámana Indians and Omoy Lume, or "Jemmy Button" — thence to the European capital, London, and again to Tierra del Fuego, and finally to Port Stanley in the Falkland (Malvinas) Islands for a final judgment. But this entire excursion is locked in the defining consciousness of Jack Guevara, who reads his own past as he writes it and measures his own destiny while he measures that of the world. What we have in this account is one of those rare pieces of fiction not only based on fact, but one which also shows insightfully and clearly the exact relation of its characters to the larger political and economic movements of the day. Like the great English 19th century novels of Thackeray, Eliot, Dickens, and Conrad, but equally in the tradition of the adventure novels of C. S. Forester, Nordhoff and Hall, and Robert Louis Stevenson, Iparraguirre concerns herself with an age of materialism, of conquest, colonialism, and imperialism. But her insights are inflected with a modern self-consciousness. Behind her also stands Borges, of whom she was a student, with his

3

ambivalence and internalized reading of reality. In him we have another Argentine produced by English and Argentine parents, the blind "Georgie" who with his Tiresian self-conscious consciousness in his own way described strange, remote worlds that inflamed the imagination:

> But here the man standing near the strait, above the dragon's tail, farther south than the flatlands and peaks of Magellan, beyond the ghostly blue mountains where men coming from the east dreamed of the enchanted valley of the immortals, the Golden City of the Caesars, ... would look stubbornly southward, in a straight line, to Cape Horn.

But these are Iparraguirre's words, not Borges'. Iparraguirre bases her story on a variety of historical sources, including Chapter 10 of Charles Darwin's *The Voyage of the Beagle* (Darwin is in fact a character in the novel) and the account of an anthropologist, Martín Gusinde, who lived with the Yámanas between 1918 and 1923. She also makes extensive use of documents she found in the public record office in London as well as the logbook of another historical personage who plays an important role in the novel, Captain Robert Fitz Roy, the commander of the Beagle, "a privileged specimen of what England had come to represent" in the year 1830 when the real action of the novel begins. This action concerns the true story of a fifteen year old Yámana Indian, Omuy Lume, who, along with three other young natives, are taken hostage by Captain Fitz Roy because one of the whaleboats has been stolen off the Beagle. As the Captain drags the naked boy aboard, he tears buttons off his officer's jacket and throws them to the canoe below by way of payment, and from this derives the English name that Omuy Lume's captors give him — Jemmy Button. The Beagle is in the Tierra del Fuego for the purpose of charting the coast, determining the navigability of its waters, and recording marine measurements of various kinds. After taking his young hostages, however, Fitz Roy does not return them. Rather, he conceives the idea of bringing the four Yámana back to London with the purpose of educating and "civilizing" them. It is this strange mission, its realization in London, its entanglement with British colonial practice in Patagonia, and the outcome of a terrible massacre of Anglican missionaries on the Isle of Keppel in the Falklands which become the central plot of Iparraguirre's novel.

Guevara asks in his journal: "Have you ever been face to face with what the books call a savage, a naked man with ribs exposed, covered with grease, his genitals swollen with disease, his face painted with streaks, and tangled, coarse hair?" This is what the youthful Jack sees when he looks at Jemmy Button for the first time. Jack has managed to snare the job of cabin boy on the Beagle with the English he has learned from his father. On ship the two boys become friends, and Jack's growing relationship with Button on shipboard, then in London, and then upon their return to the Tierra del Fuego, and even afterwards, intertwines his humanity with that of Button. The two youths circle each other, touch each other, their stories converging, paralleling each other, so that now in the present as he writes at the age of 53, Jack can in his own record correct his first youthful impression: "This is how I met Button, but it was through him that, behind such an appearance, I discovered the man I believed did not exist. And behind the man, a people with beliefs and spirit, with respect for life in all its forms, whom I had not known before and would not know again."

The personal story of Jack and Jemmy is one of bonding and separation and reunion. They share experiences in learning the ways of Victorian London and the ways of the sea and its challenges on board the Beagle both during its return to England and again on its return to Patagonia and the Tierra del Fuego — this time with the as yet unknown Charles Darwin on board. But their story emerges, it might be said, out of a larger story, a defining context captured in Fitz Roy's new mission as described by the British Admiralty: "to map the coasts of Brazil and Patagonia and study their flora and fauna. All expenses paid." As Guevara so eloquently puts it, the Admiralty's sudden granting of moneys it had in fact only recently denied "was not the product only of a love of science or altruism but of the strategic value of the Strait of Magellan and Cape Horn...." The larger contextual story of England's colonial/imperialistic intentions encompasses and blends with that of Fitz Roy's private plan to return his hostages to their homeland in order to confirm the power of the "civilizing" forces that had taught them English, dressed them in proper Victorian clothing, reduced them to a popular, sought-after diversion, and even led to their introduction to the Queen! At the very same time, on board the Beagle, the new, "modern" figure of the youthful Darwin, energetic, sharp-tongued, and furiously intelligent, challenges the backward notions of the blind if well-intentioned Captain Fitz Roy, whose misbegotten aristocratic and old-world notions garner him a self-inflicted slit throat in the end.

Iparraguirre has pointed out elsewhere that the relations between Great Britain and South America have always been conflictive, especially concerning Patagonia. Britain has long had geopolitical interest in the region and this is borne out even today by its retention of the Falklands (Malvinas) and the brief war over them as recently as 1982. It is not generally known in North America that the English attempted to take Buenos Aires in 1806 and then again in 1807. This was when Argentina was still a colony of Spain and when the Spanish and English were still struggling with each other's imperialistic designs (a struggle which goes all the way back to Renaissance times and the days of the Spanish Armada). The remote and inhospitable Tierra del Fuego and Cape Horn seem unlikely prospects for colonization and imperialistic domination in the 19th Century until one remembers that then there was no Panama Canal until the beginning of the 20th and that the only route by sea from the Atlantic to the Pacific Ocean was around Cape Horn and through the Strait of Magellan. The country which controlled this route dominated the seas in the area and thus could control all trade through it. Fitz Roy's mission on the Beagle links his own ambitions inevitably to the grander notions of the well-mannered, somber men in the Admiralty, "some in uniform and others in civilian clothes," who advance "like a procession" along its "marble floors and balustrades."

The fiction, *Tierra del Fuego*, is rooted in historical fact and is nourished by its author's consciousness of historical conditions. Equally, though conceived of as a fiction, many of its main characters are based on real people: Button, Fitz Roy, Lord Castlereagh, Darwin, the three additional Indians taken hostage, and various others. But as the author tells us: "I am not a historian. I am a writer. The novel appears to me when the fictional character appears ... And in this case this was John William Guevara. From the moment I imagined John William Guevara I had a novel. For in reality this novel is like the fictitious memories of Guevara, but these fictitious memories enter a real story, the story of Jemmy Button, his companion in the adventures of his youth. The whole story of Guevara is invented, the story of his father invented, and that of his mother too. But the real characters bring their roles in already fixed."

What are the implications of this statement? Iparraguirre seems to link her creative process to reality while insisting that the creative element is lodged in her imagination, which she pours into the consciousness of Jack Guevara as he works at his journal over a period of months, interrupting his progress from time to time with comments and descriptions concerning his daily life and the woman with whom he lives, Graciana. Reality and imagination are linked by a process of words — Iparraguirre's words, which are Jack's. It is these words, derived in part from the facts in historical documents, that make the experience real, that "bring it to life." The whole process of writing for Jack is a process of remembering and "this permits me the play of his subjectivity ... and that frees me from a historical preciousness. It is he who is remembering." One of the things that is important for Iparraguirre about this memory-prodding act of writing is that it humanizes the writer, Jack. "He becomes conscious of how Button was through this writing ... this is how writing puts in the present all that has taken place in the past. And this obliges one to reflect." Through the act of writing, Jemmy becomes real — more human — in the fullest sense. And for Iparraguirre this reflection stimulated by the act of writing is reproduced in the act of reading. It too is humanizing. At the conclusion of the book Jack determines to teach the unlettered Graciana how to read — even if she is his only reader. "Through the act of writing he begins to know her, he begins to identify her, he begins to care for her. ... So when he puts the candle on the table and begins to teach her to write, this is a positive gesture." Now she, like us, will re-experience what he wrote. And this reading, one might add, is a real process of civilization.

In this light, *Tierra del Fuego*'s wonderful descriptions of the pampa or the tumultuous sea or the mysterious land and waters of the Yámana, where the natives keep their fires alive and travel with them burning in their canoes, are not to be regarded as simply romantic decorations. Iparraguirre's notions on this subject are important:

"The descriptions in the novel create the scene. There are two major areas which are in certain ways incommensurable, one coming from the Argentine educator-president, Domingo Faustino Sarmiento, who wrote of the pampa, the other from Herman Melville, one of my favorites who affected me deeply and who wrote of the sea. But there is a third location, making, let's say, a triangle, and that is the Tierra del Fuego. And there one finds Jemmy Button. So the landscape of the pampa, or that of the sea, or that of Cape Horn, are the engines of the action. They are the places where the action develops and exposes the lives of the characters."

But the landscapes are also the sources of being of the characters whose geographies they carry in their bones just as the material world of imperialistic design shapes London and the figures it gestates. The active, physical life required of an Omoy Lume; the blank page of the pampa over which Jack Guevara broods reflecting on his life; the cool, self-justifying ambitions of Fitz Roy in London — each imbeds its character in a concrete reality long past which now only words can make real, like the words in the London Record Office or Lucín's account made real in Guevara's journal, which is the novel of *Tierra del Fuego*.

At its furthest reach *Tierra del Fuego* questions the true nature of civilization and the validity of acts often done in its name. For Argentines this inquiry finds its intellectual crux in the famous book, *Facundo, Or Civilization and Barbarism* by Domingo Faustino Sarmiento, Argentina's second president under the 1853 constitution. For the 19th Century man, Sarmiento, "barbarism meant the Indians." Iparraguirre continues, "The country's project included the price of exterminating the Indians, like what happened in the United States during the conquest of the West. They had to exterminate the owners of these lands in order to establish their own people." But the author continues that her novel is not about the "noble savage" in the Rousseauvian sense. The characters are not painted in black and white, but rather in chiaroscuro. "What I wanted to do in the novel was to look at the other side of the picture with this journey to the periphery of the world."

The picture she paints is alive with the adventures and excitement of two very different youths, Jemmy Button and Jack Guevara, who are equally comrades and competitors, and it is dense with a descriptive power often cinematic in its nature: the hot, yawning pampa, the houses and inns of Buenos

Aires beyond belief to Jack's young eyes, the thrilling port of Montevideo with its tall ships and bustling docks, London's raucous, filthy streets, the swirling, tumultuous seas in the midst of storm, the black waters of Wulaia with the fires which give the area its name flickering along its shores: Land of Fire. At the same time, the book is dramatic, like a mystery story, and actually concludes with a long trial scene derived from actual records, in which Button's true role in the terrible massacre on Cape Horn of missionaries from Keppel Island is exposed. Filled with interesting, believable, and identifiable characters, *Tierra del Fuego* is a book that readers will find difficult to put out of their minds. Furthermore, not the least of the book's accomplishments is Sylvia Iparraguirre's impressive ability to get into Jack Guevara's mind. Jack's identity as a male is complete and Iparraguirre's capacity to enter that male mind and bring it to life is thoroughly convincing. The reader never questions Jack's voice in the journal. The author's ability to adapt a 19th century writing style and use a masculine voice so unself-consciously makes one think of George Eliot. Equally, Iparraguirre has something of Eliot's capacity to enter the human soul, or psyche — its moral landscape. Indeed, above all, it is the moral landscape of the 19th century that Jack's written excursion so clearly and subtly delineates.

This moral landscape also raises important questions concerning the last part of the 20th century and the beginning of the 21st. One remembers the dilemma only recently confronted by Argentina during the so called "dirty war" of the 1970s and early 1980s, when in the name of Argentine "purity" and "Christianity" the reigning junta "disappeared" 30,000 people, forced the exile of thousands more, and ruined the lives of countless others in what can only be called a reign of terror. During this period Sylvia Iparraguirre herself was forced into "internal exile," a state in which she could not publish, suffered poverty along with her husband, the writer, Abelardo Castillo, and watched their friends endure even more terrible fates.

Notwithstanding, Iparraguirre was involved in several magazine projects. *Tierra del Fuego* thus finds a context larger than the materialism of the colonialist and imperialistic periods. It also finds a context in the immediate present. The novel may be about the Yámana, an indigenous group which has since disappeared. But, alas, it is not about a world that has disappeared. That world still survives around us, shapes us, and drives us toward our own journals of self-recognition.

*All quotations are from an interview with Sylvia Iparraguirre in Buenos Aires on February 13, 2001

The Spanish edition of *Tierra del Fuego* won the Sor Juana Inés de La Cruz award for the best work of fiction written by a woman (2000) and The Best Book of the Year Award at the Buenos Aires Book Fair (1998). Sylvia Iparraguirre has also published  two books of short stories, *In the Winter of the Cities* (1988), winner of the Municipal Prize for Literature, and *Probable Rain for the Evening* (1993), and a another novel, *The Park* (1996). She is currently working on several new works of fiction. She was born in Junín in the Province of Buenos Aires July 4, 1947 and currently lives in the city of Buenos Aires, where she is Professor of Modern Literature at the University of Buenos Aires.

Hardie St. Martin currently lives in Barcelona. In his long and distinguished career as an editor and translator, he has presented to English-speaking readers such writers as Juan Gelman, Pablo Neruda, Miguel Hernández, Blas de Otero, and others. He is editor and one of the translators of *Small Hours of the Night* by Roque Dalton (Curbstone, 1996).

*Tierra del Fuego* by Sylvia Iparraguirre • novel • 200 pages • $15.95 paper • ISBN: 1-880684-72-1

For further information, call Alexander Taylor at (860) 423-2998 or e-mail: sandy@curbstone.org

Visit Curbstone's web site at: www.curbstone.org

Curbstone Books are distributed to the trade by Consortium Book Sales and Distribution. Toll free order number: 1-800-283-3572

Winner of the

2000 Sor Juana Inés de la Cruz Prize

Sylvia Iparraguirre

# TIERRA
# del FUEGO

Translated by Hardie St. Martin

CURBSTONE PRESS

First printing: November 2000; Second printing: March 2001
Copyright © 2000 Sylvia Iparraguirre
Translation copyright © 2000 by Hardie St. Martin
All Rights Reserved

Printed in Canada on acid-free paper by Best Book Manufacturers

Cover art: "HMS 'Beagle' in Murray Narrow, Beagle Channel" by
Conrad Martens (1801-1878). Reproduced by permission from the
Bridgeman Art Library International Ltd, London & New York.

Cover design by Susan Shapiro

This book was published with major support from
Worth Loomis, as well as support from the Connecticut
Commission on the Arts, the National Endowment for
the Arts, and donations from many individuals. We are
very grateful for this support. Many thanks to Jane
Blanshard and Barbara Rosen for help in preparing the
manuscript for publication.

Library of Congress Cataloging-in-Publication Data

Iparraguirre, Sylvia.
    [Tierra del Fuego. English]
    Tierra del Fuego / by Sylvia Iparraguirre ; translated by Hardie St.
    Martin.
        p. cm.
    ISBN 1-880684-72-1
        1. Button, Jemmy, d. 1864 — Fiction. I. Title.
    PQ7798.19.P37 T5413 2000
    863'.64—dc21
    056968

published by
CURBSTONE PRESS    321 Jackson Street    Willimantic, CT 06226
        phone: (860) 423-5110        e-mail: books@curbstone.org
                    www.curbstone.org

I wish to express my gratitude to the following: to my sister Elsa Iparraguirre, a permanent source of advice; to Damián Itoiz; to Cecilia and Rex Gowar; to Oscar Zanola, Director of the Fin del Mundo Museum in Ushuaia, Tierra del Fuego; to Mercedes Güiraldes and Eduardo García Belsunce. To Irene Gruss for her careful reading of the text and to Paula Pérez Alonso for her warm encouragement. I particularly want to point out my debt to Sylvia Lodge. In London, her generous dedication of time and talent made it possible for me to obtain documents from the archives of the Public Record Office and various specialized libraries, without whose help the reconstruction of the story would have been impossible.

— Sylvia Iparraguirre

I want to thank my good friend David Unger for combing through my translated manuscript with care and for other all-round help.

— Hardie St. Martin

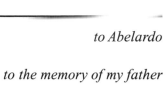

*to Abelardo*

*to the memory of my father*

"Where does what he wants to penetrate ever end? He doesn't know! What is there beyond what he can see? Solitude, danger, the savage, death!... the man who moves among these scenes is struck all at once by fears and fantastic uncertainties, dreams that preoccupy him in his waking hours."

DOMINGO SARMIENTO

"I am tormented with an everlasting itch for things remote."

HERMAN MELVILLE

# FOLIO ONE

Today, in the middle of this emptiness, something extraordinary happened. So rarely does the plain break its endless monotony that when the dot wavering on the horizon grew until it turned into a rider, and when it was obvious that these poor homes were his goal, our impatience—if watching with a quiet eye stubbornly trained on the horizon can be so called—already had us waiting for him. This was indeed something unusual, and yet watching from my house, separated from the others by a league as he came right toward us, I couldn't even dream of its true importance. The importance it would take on hours later. I say *us* thinking of the handful of scattered neighbors that make up what we call the hamlet of Lobos. About two hundred yards away I saw him turn his course westward; I could make out his profile and the horse's chestnut coat. It was noon. And then in the general store the man had asked for me. They brought him something to eat and drink and sent someone to fetch me.

A letter addressed to me in the southbound mail which rarely, if ever, turns off this way. Without dismounting, the field hand they had sent for me went on with what he had been told to say: it had to be delivered to me in person.

Before going in, I looked the man over. He seemed to be in a talkative mood. He brought news of the war with Paraguay that I fancied was partly true and partly his invention, a story that those present accepted without saying a word while filling his glass with gin from time to time, an undeclared sign that they were all ears. Before long, they noticed my presence. The man stood up and wiped his mouth with the back of his hand: "Are you the English major?"

Before I could answer, the old man, back in his usual corner at the rear of the store, said, "No. The major was his father, the gringo. This is our friend, Guevara, that's all."

In common Argentine speech my father's English

surname—Mallory—had ended up becoming *májori** first, and afterwards, oddly enough, *major*, a rank in the army, but I said nothing.

People around here are clannish and not overly curious, and yet for my uncultured neighbors the letter and the letter's delivery itself, as well as the man's whole procedure, solemn in its way, of searching the saddlebag and digging out these yellowish papers, much handled and sealed; of watching me as if he had to make sure of a connection between my face and what he was putting in my hands, or as if my unresponsive attitude, I suppose, made him doubt that I was the one it was addressed to, all held something mysterious about it. Everyone present looked at the papers sealed and lacquered with the suspicion common to illiterates, the way you look at something likely to set off a chain of unpredictable events.

Now I can assure you that the letter, the man who appeared and disappeared on the plain, and the things I've just explained are beginning to slip indifferently into oblivion. Here in Lobos the monotony of the days is like a slow, powerful river that wears away events until they're reduced to a polished stone, later on a grain of sand, and finally nothing. In my case, at least, the result suspected by my neighbors was fulfilled, and the letter did, in fact, produce an unpredictable change. As proof of this turn, let me point out something completely unrelated to the natural order of my days that is taking place before my eyes, on this table: the act of writing or my determination to write.

When the messenger left and was once more swallowed up by the prairie, I galloped home, broke the seals and lacquers, and read the words from the other side of the ocean. I read and reread the letter, over and over again. That afternoon I picked up my pipe and tobacco and left the house. I walked

* In Argentina, "ll" is prounced like the letter "j".

4

deep into the prairie where the sky's vault rules and over-powers one. Overhead, a sky of the purest blue; below, the prairie like a flat circle. My dog Ajax is my sole witness. The wind sweeps the dry earth. High above, a flock of cormorants cuts through the air. I returned and shut myself in my house. Once again I read what I now translate: *...since you were a privileged and direct witness of those events, we would like you to draw up a thorough account of that voyage and of the subsequent fate of the ill-starred native who took part as leader of the slaughter for which he has been tried in the Islands.*

The letter stirred up a growing uneasiness in me. Which was the apt version required in the case of the "ill-starred native," the man called Jemmy Button by the English but whose real name, his Yámana name, almost no one ever knew? The Indian in top hat, with cheekbones shining under the top hat, wearing a frock coat, a kind of coachman, stubby and gro-tesque, a Button, submissive and smiling, tossing coins into the air above the grimy paving stones of London? Or the savage from Cape Horn, naked under the icy rain, with his body stinking of seal grease, the part in his hair nonexistent and his face smeared black? Or, in the end, the aging and impassive man I saw again years later on the bench for the accused during the trial in the Islands, whose eyes, fearless in their sunken sockets, looked for the last time at the whites, the white men who came from the east? Yes, Jemmy Button's fate had taken a strange turn since the captain had taken him hostage in exchange for some mother-of-pearl buttons, but there had been no "subsequent fate" for the "ill-starred native."

Yet over and above all, the letter raised other questions in me. How had they found me? And, assuming that they had known how to find me, why had the letter been delayed six months, when two, at most, would have been more normal?

5

It had not been forced open; I was the first to know its contents. Having discarded this possibility, I visualized the letter's itinerary: Liverpool or Plymouth, the Cape Verde Islands, possibly the Azores, Brazil, the port of Montevideo, Buenos Aires. At some point on the foreseeable route, blind chance had stepped in. Chance and monotony are the ocean's two constants. The mail bag must have been forgotten under merchandise meant for more urgent delivery. Or else it had been unloaded in the midst of some mix-up at a previous port. Or, in all likelihood, what had no doubt occurred was something else: it had arrived without mishap in Buenos Aires—the only address written on it, with the exception of my name—where it had been forgotten for months. This was more than possible, quite typical of this country whose indolence, like its rivers and trees, is part of the natural order of things, that after such a sea passage, the letter should remain for months only a few leagues from its final destination.

In defense of my countrymen, I should say that people at the port know me well, but it has been a few years since I returned to live in my country. To all this I must add that, with a war on our northern border for which the government shows great enthusiasm, who was going to worry about a letter to an unknown person, to a man not even at the front? This is my explanation: with the letter delayed in the port of Buenos Aires, someone just happened to recognize my name and put it in the southbound mail.

At nightfall, oppressed by the walls, I went out into the corridor and let the darkness slowly close around me. My thoughts took a leap from the present to the past, rushing blindly, because the news of the Captain's death, also brought by the letter, had hit me like a tremendous blow on the back; a demise signed at the bottom, with the seals of the British Admiralty, by you, Mr. MacDowell or MacDowness. I can't quite make out your name where the paper is folded and this,

I presume, must mean something. The ornate seal and the many ups and downs the letter has been through prevent me from making out your signature clearly. And even more disappointingly, just as I can't decipher the letters in your name, I cannot give that name a face. An unfamiliar face thousands of miles away, in one of the Admiralty's countless stuffy offices. It's one place, at least, I can recall in detail. I got to know the marble passageways and the coffered ceilings below which the Captain spoke warily to the owners of the Empire, and I also got to know the lesser installations where lowly clerks await orders. I assume that you belong among the second.

And yet if your face and the table on which the letter was written were to vanish into thin air, the paper, on the other hand is real, I can touch it. The words are precise and are addressed to me, they have come to look for me at the other end of the world, and they drag me back to the past with the force of a strong gale from the sea. The weight (should I say instead *the burden*?) is definitely borne by the final words: under the seals and lacquers, these simple words about the Captain that I translate: *we are sorry to inform you that he took his life, cutting his throat with his own razor exactly three days ago, on April 30, 1865.* These final words, so oddly precise, and perhaps even deliberate, in an official letter, aside from their purport, moved me deeply, since the Captain is of that breed of men whom one cannot imagine dead, much less with their throats cut by their own hand, a breed to which my own father belonged.

The event, which had occurred months ago, was now happening for me, was taking place before my eyes in the absolute present time of this letter: the Captain, such as I remembered him with indelible clarity, in his residence near London, in the dressing room adjoining his bedroom, in front of his mirror, was about to make the calm gesture of taking up the razor. At sea I had often seen him show that composure at desperate moments. A coldness that deep down was the self-sufficiency of extreme pride. Here I was, powerless, watching him raise the razor, seeing him move his arm across and press the blade below his left ear with mad precision, the other hand gripping the elbow so the arm cannot refuse. I saw the sudden movement, the horrified leap of the blood onto the mirror, the body's heavy fall, the corpse on the floor, no doubt dressed in a naval uniform. Or perhaps *in his naval uniform* is something I like to imagine.

The Captain was not a man to stay on land. There is something I must point out in advance, Mr. MacDowell or MacDowness, something that includes me. The sea is an excess and men given to sailing share a kind of madness that those who have always remained on land can never manage to understand. Days and nights at sea are not measured by days and nights but by the unrelievable fatigue that follows the struggle with the storm, by the desolate plunge of a corpse into the ocean, by scurvy or fever, by the splendor of the mornings, by the movement of the stars among the triumphant masts.

The letter acts on me like a kind of poison, like that drink in the Fiji Islands that, amazingly, placed before one's eyes images of a hallucinatory tenacity from which one could not awaken or come out of or break free. With the night already pitch-black, I went inside, lit the lamp and the candles, poured myself a glass of wine, arranged pen and ink on the table, and wrote what I am copying now: *My dear sirs: Your letter reaches me five months after its London date. I don't know what the fate of mine will be or in what way I can help you with the events you ask me to narrate. Events so remote in time that I do not know if I shall be able to recount them in detail...*

These lines on a loose sheet of paper are my only formal attempt to answer your letter, Mr. MacDowell or Mac-Downess.

The first thing that comes to mind is the fire perforating the darkest night of the planet, fires devoured by wild gusts of wind that made anyone looking on from the ship's rail dumb with suspense and fear.

Between 64° and 70° longitude west of the Greenwich meridian and parallels 52° and 56° of the southern latitude, the last fragment of South America extends: Tierra del Fuego, the *Terra Incognita Australis,* wide open, broken up into islands and interminable channels so that if a man stood on the northern coast of the Strait of Magellan facing south, before him in a straight line only a few miles away he would see the extreme tip of this formation—the continent's southernmost islands—Cape Horn, where oceans furiously converge. Behind him, on his back, the man would be carrying South, Central and North America, with their tropics, their Equator, with all their rivers, jungles, and mountains, all the way to Alaska. But standing here, in this hemisphere, at the edge of the strait, should the man lift his face to the heavens, overhead he would be able to watch the legendary beauty of the Southern Cross, priceless jewel for mariners from the North, and then, should the man open his arms in imitation of the constellation he has been gazing at, should he open them all the way, his left hand would point to the mouth of the strait for which, terrified and lost, the Spaniards longed, and to the coasts that Pigaffeta named *the land of the fires* for the reddish chain of bonfires with which the country's inhabitants warned each other of the passing of enormous strange beings with humps and tree-like growths which coursed through the water but were not whales. At the same time, his outstretched right hand would point to the mountains in the west, the range which, coming down from the north, sinks and surfaces again on the large island to run over it, slanting like the last stretch of the black and burned dragon's tail whose rocky tip comes up for the last time on the Isle of States, and which, rising again northward with its colossal spine sticking out across the length of different climates, twists around at the height of the shoulder blades to pounce voraciously on the Caribbean sea at the green delta of the Orinoco. But here the man standing near the strait, above the dragon's tail, farther south than the flatlands and peaks of Magellan, beyond the ghostly blue mountains where men coming from the east dreamed of the enchanted valley of the immortals, the Golden City of the Caesars, the man would look stubbornly southward, in a straight line, to Cape Horn.

Two hundred miles farther down, the glaze of mist breaks open and the rain comes down on the last islands, the ever-lasting wind lifts gigantic icy waves, and foam flies in all directions. Cape Horn, site of shipwrecks where seamen, haunted by the dire reputation of this point where oceans seem to meet in combat, and by the obsessive thought of losing their way in the maze of islands and channels wrapped in eternal mist, believed they could hear the moans of the drowned, the murmurs of those shipwrecked centuries ago who seemed to call out, begging for help from coasts covered in gloom. The terrifying vision one morning of a sail rigid in the grip of ice that we sailors started to pound as if we were attempting to break an evil spell. Furthermore, what comes back to me is not what I later learned or saw of those places, their quiet little harbors where red trees bent over and where fires were reflected like stars, but my first deceptive impression as a greenhorn sailor. This unchanging scene appears most often: a group of men on deck, numb with cold, and the Captain among them, watching out for the slightest trace of the coast and its fires, knowing—as I do now—deep in his heart that this inexplicable yearning, a mixture of fear and determination, was born of his conscience, his pride, or the guilt skirting the secret limits of the world.

I was eighteen years old, and I was also there. In the same place where John Byron, the famous poet's grandfather, had sailed and founded the first English settlement in the Islands that another Englishman had given the name of Falkland, without caring about the hundred-year-old treaty. The Islands which more than a century before Anson had considered the key to the South Seas, the Islands the Captain marked out following express secret instructions from the Admiralty. But, especially for me that night, the Islands where thirty years later I would see Jemmy Button alone for the last time and where I took leave forever of his inscrutable Yámana face.

One thing leads me to another. I am not in the habit of writing. My thoughts move faster than my pen, and the order of these paragraphs is not, I believe, accurate. Words are like wild horses that rush out blindly in stampede, banding together, following one another.

I don't believe that what I am writing is the kind of account you request, Mr. MacDowell or MacDowness. All at once I feel sure of it. I wouldn't be telling the truth if I said it matters to me.


It's two in the morning. Graciana is asleep in her cot. I replace the stub of candle in order to go on. The wind has dropped and the peaceful, universal night takes over everything. From my window the pampa in the moonlight is a vastness that evokes nothingness first of all and quiet fear after that. No one, with the exception of reckless persons and a few gauchos, would venture into that silence. Now and then groups of giant carts bent with weight move across the horizon like lost ships. If I mention the prairie, it is because for me it is still something recovered. I was born and raised on it, I left just as I was beginning to live, and now that I have returned I need to name it. My countrymen never think about this place, they simply live in it.

The letter says: *The Royal Navy, in which you served England with honour, will be grateful for this last service that it now requests of you...*

How the devil the Royal Navy ever found me is one of the questions that will remain unanswered. My arrival in the Islands took place, I am sure, completely unnoticed by the authorities. You're not ignorant of the fact that I am the son of an Argentine mother and an English father, and, as on so many other occasions in my life, it was my appearance and the English language that allowed me to attend Button's trial like just another American.

Setting foot on the Islands, as you well know, Mr. MacDowell or MacDowness, is forbidden to all the inhabitants of the Argentine Confederation.

Nevertheless, Great Britain seems to know everything. Perhaps its information about my whereabouts goes back many years. Perhaps a former fellow seaman questioned by you people in London told you of my intention to come back and settle in my place of birth, this country which I'm not ashamed to call my own. Perhaps you suspect that I was not unaware of the objectives of that first passage about which your letter asks for a report, that I knew the secret instructions given the Captain about the strategic value of Argentina's Patagonia and the Islands...

You are mistaken, Mr. MacDowell or MacDowness. I learned much later what I know now.


What I have written may give the impression that mine has been an isolated life. That has not been the case. If indeed I live alone—the presence of a few field hands and Graciana, the young Argentine who works for me and lives in the house, doesn't count—, from 1858, the year I returned to Lobos to rebuild this house, I have been in sporadic contact with the world through the port of Buenos Aires. My last trip to the Islands and my presence at the trial are directly related to my visits to the port and my information about ships and captains, Captain Smyley among them. I don't mind confessing —I ask myself to whom—that I have been in frequent contact with sailors off seal-hunting vessels and whalers that go down south all the time. From them I was not amazed to learn of the English missionaries massacred by the Yámanas and of the investigation ordered by Governor Moore on the Islands, which the Mission's members also had to attend.

There is nothing stranger than that trial on the desolate Islands I had known as a twenty-year-old in the company of the Captain and the "little doctor" and which even then many called the Malouinas after the good French mariners of Saint Malo. Three hundred and fifty miles from Tierra del Fuego, the wind went on sweeping the deserted beaches with the same indifferent savagery as almost thirty years before. I relived the same oppressive feeling. It springs from the solitude, the trees clinging to the earth with difficulty, bent over in the wind's direction, causing the sensation of almost physical punishment. I went off for a walk along the rocky beach in order to think. The wind brought me the strong whiff of a colony of sea lions living on the small peninsula at the bay's entrance. The hoarse cries the corpulent males hurl to the sky came to me from there. Suddenly I felt the knife-like cold of the climate in my bones again. I was grateful for the shelter of the houses which now formed a small village and were new to me.

For some reason, since the *Kimberley,* the whaler on which I shipped out, had turned its prow to the south, and I saw the tall coasts of the Patagonia cliffs, the passage began to take on the dreamlike quality of something unreal. Far from abating, this sensation had increased when I stepped ashore and would only cease abruptly two days later when I found myself alone, face to face with Button.

I was on my way back to the houses and I remember the

feeling of incredulity that paralyzed me at the prospect of seeing my old companion. In the end, our encounter in the fog four years before had not been the last. As in the past, once again we were two strangers in a world that mistrusted us. What would happen to Button? What would he do when he saw me? This had been the only thing on my mind since I left Buenos Aires. In Port Stanley the subject of every conversation was Button, the accused, and Alfred Coles, the only survivor of the massacre.

I confess that I traveled to the Islands for the sole purpose, the secret intention of helping him, of testifying in his favor if it was necessary. I wasn't sure how I would justify my presence, but this was my real intention though no one knew it. Now I am writing it down, leaving written evidence, Mr. MacDowell or MacDowness.

That night in Port Stanley, the eve of the trial, was a very long one, shared in part with my old acquaintance Captain Smyley, commander of the *Nancy*, the schooner which had brought the prisoner from Tierra del Fuego. The wind howled steadily in the stone fireplace, beside which I had settled myself, and it depressed me. I was thinking of what Smyley had told me. Here would be the "ill-starred savage" who had come of his own free will from Cape Horn to testify, a man forty-six years old, with his rudimentary and guttural English, facing the administration's officials. The cause: the bloody deeds, "the massacre" his tribe had supposedly carried out under his leadership.

It is easy to guess—I must correct myself—, that wakeful night it was easy for me to guess that the Yámanas had become fed up with the English and their missions. The white men, the men who came from the east, had invaded their lands, raped their women and young girls, killed their animals. They had forced them to wear clothes and work and had separated the children from their parents. It was also easy for me to guess that the English could not flatly accept their failure. Years back, people had become excited about the mission reserved for England: to evangelize and educate. The effort made in that remote and hostile climate, the English society's goodwill, the notices in the newspapers, and even the interest of the royal couple had come to this: a barbaric act of massacre.

The hopes placed in a savage trained in the ways and languages of civilization had resulted in murder. The Yámanas had killed them all. They had smashed in their skulls with rock after rock and had later gone on board ship and stolen everything. Not even nails had they left on board the *Allen Gardiner,* which remained there, silent and ghostly, pitching and rolling adrift in a small bay near the Strait of Murray. In effect, they had murdered them all. Coles, the ship's cook, had been the only one saved. And Coles would also be there as the only witness to the facts. Poor devil: in London there were hundreds like him, cannon fodder the cities vomit into the ports—that's what was said—confronting Button with his version. Coles, I had been told, was partly out of his mind. The three months of captivity among the Yámanas had left him in a state little short of madness. They were all there in the presence of Governor Moore, the deacon, and the Island's notables. All under a huge billboard that appeared spontaneously and went round and round in my head before I fell asleep: the British Empire versus Jemmy Button.

And there I was again, Mr. MacDowell or MacDowness, next to Button as I had been thirty years before. Someone under false pretenses amidst settlers and mariners. Like everyone, but for different reasons more than anyone else, I was impressed by Button's presence. A good while must have elapsed before I was able to recover and take in what I was seeing. Why not say it, I felt a violent thrill of happiness when I saw him sit down without any show of fear in the seat of the accused, without even suspecting that back among those present was his old friend and buddy. The past and my lost youth gnawed at my mind. All I can say is that this

Yámana, who had been decently covered with English clothes but was still in his bare feet, this self-assured, aging man who carried fire in his canoe and lived in a labyrinth of islands at the world's end, this man had stared at me once on a ship's deck as astonished and cautious as I was staring at him now. We had sailed in early youth on an endless ocean and had discovered together a world whose existence neither of us had even suspected. All this, thirty years ago.

The letter came more than a week ago, and I find that the act of sitting down to write has ordered my life in a singular way. Nowadays Graciana's silent presence has taken on the semblance of a question. She looks at me without understanding what it is that keeps me bent over the table, or why I don't go to her. Perhaps you realize, Mr. MacDowell or MacDowness, at the age of fifty-three the need for a woman can easily be put off till later on.

It dawns on me that writing in the daytime by natural light and writing at night by candlelight are different things. In the daytime I feel the urge to talk about the house and everyday things, and I have even overcome, like now, the objection to talking about such insignificant things as, for example, that at this very moment the wall back there is lit up by the setting sun, something slight but unique that I cannot stop admiring. Toward evening I gradually fall prey to the unconquerable melancholy of the pampa, and at night I grow feverish, as if I were not writing but fighting off something. At that hour innumerable images I don't want to talk about appear, things that I have seen or lived and reappear as if demanding not to be excluded from this narrative: sad brothels in Madagascar, trees centuries old whose invincible roots break through the walls of abandoned temples, islands that look like Paradise, the nightmarish bedlam of ports astir with humanity.

But even if this has nothing to do with this story, there is something I must point out.

During these days of silence and spontaneous celibacy I have been thinking. I've had to take stock. It has been inevitable.

For many years I have lived in the middle of events, within History. Now I am on the sidelines, and I can analyze things from the past the way one analyzes a piece of writing. I am not defending any position; embarked on a war which does not concern me and which I condemn, my countrymen literally give me the cold shoulder. No one has eyes for the South. In this sense, I feel lost, like a foreigner. Fortunately I am not a public man. I don't have to justify my actions in writing. My life is my own and concerns only me, so much so that no one seems to be aware of my existence. Which, then, are the events I took part in and which after all these years are worth bringing out into the light? The expedition of the Captain on his way to investigate and draw notice to the Patagonian coasts in the year 1829. As you know, this was not his only goal. In my modest opinion, there are two ways of seeing this undertaking: one, with the progress of civilization in mind, the privilege of men who make history. In this case the end justifies the means, for it is a matter of taking the light of learning to lands and human beings sunk in darkness. It is a noble end; in consequence, the means may not matter.

A different reading is contrary to the so-called philanthropy of the men from the east (that's how the inhabitants of Tierra del Fuego referred to them and what Button called them). In this way of seeing things, the alleged civilizing intention turns into a different kind of barbarism, more refined than the barbarism that resorts to arms, more cunning. The only motto of this behavior may be stated thus: "Everything fits in with the ends, yes; whatever doesn't fit in must be changed, reduced, or eliminated." *The ends* must read *our ends*. This has been one of my motives for reflection.

An entirely different one is that, stimulated by your letter, in order to bring them up to the present, my memory seems to lump together or superimpose events that are far apart or of a different nature. What you ask me to tell has to do not only with what I saw or lived through but also with things I read or was told. Recalled are endless nights at sea filled with old stories of shipwrecks, in keeping with a tradition, and which at the same time instilled terror in the heart of a cabin boy, perhaps preparing him for the life ahead of him. Remote stories of Spaniards or Dutchmen already woven into legend or recent events, backed up with precise details, or specific events like stumbling upon Melville's book during the harsh winter that held us up in New York, the winter of 1853. Wandering through city streets, I came upon a book-store and in it the volume that has been with me ever since. Sitting in an inn near the waterfront, where some of my companions and I had taken our things until the snow blew over, by the grey light of three in the afternoon, so dim that I had to ask for a lamp to read by, I opened the book and was unable to close it again until four days later, when I turned the last page. The vision of the painting the author places in the tavern in New Bedford was always with me: behind the counter, obscured by time and smoke, the painting never ceased to arouse fear in anyone who looked at it. In the midst of ice floes and mountainous waves, a whale, with the unlimited fury of all its power, attacks a ship about to be torn apart and dragged to the bottom of the ocean's abyss. And this was at Cape Horn; the scene spoken of in the book was taking place where I had been on countless occasions, cruising in icy fog among islands where one day the Captain had taken Button hostage, paid for him with a button, and had him brought up on deck.

I have let several days go by without writing. If I start again it's because I have definitely rid myself of a question that, once I had started this account—or whatever you may choose to call it—, pounced on me like a dog on its prey. In what language should these words be written? In this one that I call mine, or in that of the letter, in other words, yours? As you can see, I selected mine in order to carry out this senseless act whose very lack of sense impels me to carry it out. Or perhaps because every story should have its own writer and I no longer wish to tell what you ask me to but what I wish to tell, as if in some mysterious way your letter has opened a floodgate and behind it all I have lived had been waiting for an opportunity like this. I have never thought of myself as a typical man of the sea but it goes without saying that sailors are fond of telling stories.

As it is, the decision or instinct to use my maternal and not my paternal tongue cancels beforehand any possible communication. Therefore I am not writing for you, Mr. MacDowell or MacDowness with your unfamiliar face, or even for the British Admiralty. On the other hand, where I live, the flat line of the horizon works against any kind of action, makes it useless. Nor do I write for my countrymen, the people of these plains, who know nothing about the southern tip of our country where these things happened.

For my own solace, I've come to understand that the act of writing justifies itself and requires no explanation. In spite of having spent two thirds of my life at sea, I am a well-read man; but between London and unrefinement, for better or for worse, I chose refinement. Civilization and savagery tend to go hand in hand. The same thing is true of writing and unrefinement, as shown by the famous Dampier, almost as good a pirate as a writer. I hasten to make it clear that my pretensions are not that lofty. What are they? I'm not sure right now. I must nevertheless acknowledge something: I am indebted to England for the books I've read.

In short, thirty-five years ago, in 1830, I was a member of the English expedition that carried Button and three other native Indians, among them a young girl, from Cape Horn to London. Two years later I embarked on the following expedition, which returned them to their country. For several years I continued to serve in the Royal Navy and later on the ships of other nations. Tired of the sea, eight years ago I returned to my homeland. One day, I learned about the massacre of the English missionaries blamed on Button's tribe and supposedly led by him, Jemmy Button, and his son Billy. Five years ago, at the beginning of 1860, I was a witness at his trial in the Islands, where I had landed secretly, and where I saw him and spoke to him for the last time. Last year I heard that he had died during a smallpox epidemic. I don't know the Admiralty's motive in asking for this account. There has to be one. I know that Great Britain does not act without a motive. Whatever it was, it does not concern or touch me in any way. This is my story and it belongs to me. From now on I pass over this letter and its ulterior designs.

Having said this, before I go on it may be relevant to this story to say who I am.

# FOLIO TWO

Saying who I am means talking about the sea. Many years before ever getting a glimpse of the sea, I knew it was my destiny, as it was the destiny of the main character of the book with which my father, William Scott Mallory, taught me to read. The sea, his voice and the English language indiscernibly joined forces in the first years of my life. Of my mental life, I should say. Everpresent in my early roots, in my food, in the wind, in the horses, and on the plain, are my mother, Lucía de Guevara, and the Spanish language.

Be that as it may, I have been delaying the moment to write my name. My name is a hybrid. I can't help feeling the violent effect its introduction will have on what I write.

My last name is my mother's: Guevara. My first names, John William, were left up to my father and he simplified them to Jack. My father's insistence on my being given English names was, I admit, odd, while he did not mind that my last name should be left up to my mother, whom he never married. I regard this as another sign of his basic uprootedness, of his enigmatic vocation to belong nowhere in particular, to leave no heir or family name.

I notice a certain symmetry between you and me, Mr. MacDowell or MacDowness, between your letter and what I write. I can't figure out your name; mine must have puzzled you. Who, then, is the one writing? I'll say it another way, or from another point of view, conceded now by the name already down on paper: the one who recalls these events and writes is John William Guevara, fifty-three years old, born in a part of the flatlands of what today is called the Argentine Confederation. He was brought up in a primitive country, far from almost everything, speaks and writes two languages, and has unknowingly adopted a kind of double identity. His mother's: Argentine, Roman Catholic, devout; his father's: English, Protestant, blaspheming. The melding of languages gave him certain involuntary tendencies: toward the elemental and steadfast on his mother's side; toward uprootedness and melancholy on his father's. Consequently, in terms of belief, he is a skeptic, and in terms of character, a loner who at the age of seventeen left the plain behind him and went to sea.

My mother was a delicate, dark-complexioned woman, with high cheekbones and big dark eyes. Except for a strict Catholic education, her parents had not thought any further study was necessary and she barely knew how to read and write. My father used to say that she suffered from "fanatic servility" toward the priests, whom he detested. She had a rather bewildered, insecure look. She would stare at me long and hard, as if it was difficult to believe in the miraculous mutation that made a son of hers, as she said, have "hair the color of sand" and grey eyes. She would often take me astride her mare's haunches to buy candles or sugar at the country store. In the half-light inside, thick with the raw smell of sheep's leather and candle grease, they would make me speak English. For a five- or six-year-old boy to speak "furrin" was as rare as a prodigy or a freak in a country fair. They would stand me up on a barrel top and command:

"Talk in gringo, talk in gringo!"

At first I would play dumb, and then, perhaps spurred on by the sudden attention to my person, I would start to thread together loose phrases and to name objects in the place. Each word was cheered with exclamations and outbursts of laughter, which made my mother, upset, come to my rescue, to save me from those gatherings of laughing ruffians who, upon hearing me, went back to a past fresh in their memory, deeds of blood that had happened years ago, before my birth, and with which they shared something heroic that I couldn't understand although they told me about it, as if wanting to win me over to their cause. Years later I understood it: I, the son of a gringo and an Argentine woman, was living proof that the war between the English and the Argentines had had other developments, less spectacular and predictable, less public, and, for that reason, perhaps more disquieting.

I grew up with two languages. My mother's and my father's. They understood each other almost without words. Sometimes one of them accepted monosyllables or a short phrase from the other's language. But only now and then and in extreme circumstances. As if they did it against their will, as if the one who yielded with that foreign accent were confessing guilt or if in doing it they were reviving, inside the house walls, the war I mentioned. But my mother's English was much better than my father's Spanish. Clumsy syllables, badly put together, came from him and it was only well after one started listening to them that it became obvious that they were meant to be Spanish.

Lucía de Guevara died when I was ten years old. I believe now that her illness sprang from her having run away with a foreigner, an English invader. And yet, for her, the ordeal by fire must have been her having become a heretic's mistress. She had been poisoned from the pulpit by hysterical priests who thundered out stories of pacts between heretics and Satan, and these led my mother, even as a child, to believe— and this was never disproved—that the English were Lutherans who, like the Devil, had tails. Fate had reserved for her the paradox of having to solve the enigma for herself by falling in love with an Englishman. An aftertaste of this legend of anathema hovered around Mallory. And as if to confirm it to anyone who would listen, he used to say that the Spanish priests feared the Devil less than English commerce and dominion which would make them lose their church benefits, their big paunches, and their whores.

I don't think I've said anything important, Mr. Mac-

Dowell or MacDowness, for in those years my father, your countryman, was invariably drunk.

The story of his traffic with the Devil, in addition to his being a heretic, grew because he became famous for never losing his way on the plain. A gaucho never gets lost in the desert because at night he sleeps with his head pointing in the direction he is going. My father slept on the ground just like on a canopied bed and in any position. He never lost his way. There was no supernatural aptitude or magic in this. Besides being familiar with the stars, he owned a compass that, among my fellow countrymen, was considered an artifact brought straight from Hell.

A sailor chooses his country, and I chose mine. If at any point in my past I felt like a foreigner, it was not for myself but for Mallory; whenever, as a small boy, I would hear the words "that shit of an Englishman" or "gringo drunkard" used in order to name him. Words that I believe he began by not understanding and ended up not hearing.

I remember one night when he heard and understood them. The man who said them found himself flat on his back on the store's floor after my father's backhand blow. When he got up he had a knife in his hand. The oil lamp hanging from a beam was swinging over our heads, and the shadows crawled up the walls where the arm and the knife seemed enormous. I don't know if it was Mallory's look, since he now had a grip on a bottle's neck and didn't budge an inch, because he had the reputation of being crazy, or all of this together, but the other man backed into a corner and slipped like a shadow through the open door into the dark. In the silence that followed, the gallop of the horse plunging into the plain mingled with my father's breathing, like a bellows slowly getting back its wind.

What fixed this episode in my mind wasn't the fight itself so much as the certainty that, if I had stepped in, Mallory would not have recognized me and might even have slit my throat then and there. His eyes that night revealed to me a man I didn't know or had not yet fully known. Just as, years later, I discovered that fights didn't scare him; he had had hundreds in London's taverns and in those of the many ports he must have touched, and yet he disliked violence. When it came to fighting, he told me once, an overwhelming laziness came over him, and it was this reluctance that he had to shake off in order not to look like a coward. Neither of the two scars on his body came from hand-to-hand fighting. One of these he had acquired when during a storm he rescued a sailor hanging from the bowsprit. The other, on the upper floors of a London tavern in not very heroic circumstances.

Deep down William Scott Mallory was a peace-loving, indolent man who loved to pamper animals, which scandalized people in this country and increased his fame as an eccentric. In those days, during my early years, I feared and observed him from a safe distance. He always went around with a dog at his heels; three or four of them invariably slept under his cot or on top of it, and they trailed him everywhere like loyal bodyguards. Once I saw him patting a calf on the back and I believe even talking to it in English; he said he was doing it to tame him, but he may have been drunk at the time.

We lived in isolation, outside this village, on a piece of land purchased from the government, and in this house which he wanted to build himself like those in Europe, that is, with bricks ordered from I don't know where, since they were not made here, and windows with glass panes, which are unknown in houses in the country. He was an Englishman who wanted to keep in this land some of the advantages of civilization. The house is modest but in those days it seemed, and still seems today, superior to the adobe houses with thatched roofs and no windows. It has a fireplace, unheard of here, that he insisted on building, as if by means of it he could recover even only a very tiny part of his distant country.

"Drunk but civilized!" he would say when my mother reproached him for drinking. He would refer to the luxuries I have mentioned, which no one here could understand. In the middle of all this, one thing was certain, finding my father sober was something rare. Sober or drunk, in the light of the oil lamp he would talk about England and the sea.

His being in this remote country was incongruous at first but ended up as something natural. Some years after the British defeat or Argentine victory, the indifference of the settlers swallowed like silent quicksand everything William Scott Mallory had of stranger, gringo, or even invader. His foreignness was reduced to sly disdain whenever anyone saw my father do something awkward as far as local ways went. In any case, after that fight no one ever interfered with the gringo again. Mallory had won the respect of my countrymen.

It is still some time before daybreak, Mr. MacDowell or MacDowness. The bottle has been emptied and my pipe is cold. I open the window to let the night's freshness clear the stale air as well as my head. Perhaps you'd like to remind me that the reason for this is Jimmy Button, not my life. I'm not forgetting him; I assure you I can't put him out of my mind. But it's my life story that takes me to him, as decades ago his path accidentally crossed mine. Events, people, and the demands and duties of navigation aside, a long time ago Button's destiny assumed the form of mine.

The almost zoological distance I felt between us when I saw him for the first time was followed by a gradual understanding of his world that only maturity was able to complete, when Button was already far away, in the ultimate corner of the earth. There had been nights in the tropics, lying on deck, rocked by a calm sea, our eyes on the swift clouds that let us glimpse the stars as big as fists, nights when I believed we were two young men drunk with the same exalted feeling of being at one with the world. I couldn't see then that Button's was a hand-to-mouth existence. It's possible that

I saw only the picturesque side, the odd side of the savage on board ship. It is also possible, almost certain, that I still considered myself almost an Englishman and superior to him, and consequently I believed that my feelings were his, as if he had no right to have his own. He struggled with English, paradoxically the only language in which we could communicate. The long crossing and the heat wore him down, and all he talked about were things in his icebound country that he was leaving farther and farther behind, farther south. He soon understood, in his relations with the men from the east, that obeying meant food, something very scarce and difficult to come by in his country and which the white men seemed to dispose of in amazing quantities.

Now Jemmy Button is dead. Tried by the white men who took away all his sustenance and in the end showed they had never considered him a man, Button rests at Cape Horn. His adventure has been swallowed up by the ice and the wind at the end of the world. But I remember it. For some reason I can't fathom, my life's story cannot be explained without his.

Jemmy Button cannot be summed up by the day on which the Captain took him aboard as hostage or by the occasions on which he pointed out to me the beauty of his country, of which he was so proud. Nor can he be reduced to our passage to England nor to the prophetic meeting in the fog; nor even to the aged figure I ran into thirty years later in the Islands. Time and experience filled in his story.

Over the years, news of Button would come from the most unlikely places to find me. It's something natural. My life was spent among men of the sea, in taverns in ports or on islands of replenishment where one ship or another would always come after sailing around Cape Horn. They were like weak signals that he still existed and would reappear in my life. Those skimpy rumors were always the best excuse for me to call for another bottle and maybe that's why, for some days now, there's always been one next to me on this table.

In the harbors of Tasmania or Africa, Button's distant echo would reach my ears, once more looking for me. Sometimes they were more than echoes. Once, on the island of Mauritius, in a warehouse in port, I found a bundle of old newspapers. Having a newspaper at hand was an unusual treat that seldom came one's way. It was like holding on to something, confirming the memory that in some places men still followed the custom of keeping within bounds of what was said there. Above all, they had the unique taste of the news report, no matter that it was out of date. For someone who hasn't been on land for a long time, it means catching up, belonging once more in the company of men. The news was from London, back in 1834, and, surprisingly, it had something to do with me. The English press was indignant at what had been done to the Yámanas. It criticized the Captain for having abandoned them again on Cape Horn after giving them education in England. At first I was surprised; and then the others couldn't understand why I should burst out laughing.

I'll explain, Mr. MacDowell or MacDowness, what I had to explain to my companions that time. I had also been among those who had taken Button and the others back to their country. Further on I'll tell what that really meant; at the moment I only laughed. The fact that English society was indignant now, after approving their being taken away from London—what's finally to be done with Indians?—, could only make me laugh. They had amused themselves with them for some time, had literally smothered them with junk, and had rewarded their patience with ridiculous gifts. From every nook and corner of England there had come teapots, tablecloths, and silverware for the homes that, imitating those in London, the British imagined the Yámanas would build at the world's end. Do you know how the Yámanas live? Have you seen a wigwam between the beach and the forest tied down to the rocks during a storm? Do you even know what a wigwam is? Well, there was something else, something more interesting that I should tell you.

A year after returning Button to his country dressed in top hat, frock coat, and gloves, the Captain—on his way past Cape Horn again—decided to look for him, and of course we found him. That figure appeared before us on deck once more, with nothing left of the clothes or the good English nourishment of twelve months back, but in whom one could see the strange self-assurance, the unusual importance that Button had definitely always had for the whites. Naked, so thin you could count his ribs, and his skin speckled with white paint, but with a gleam of human determination in his eyes, he proudly said no. He did not want to return to England. He would never return. I recall his wife's screams in their canoe; hardly more than a child, she was terrified that he would leave her. I recall that, as he left the ship, I tried to hug him good-bye. All he did was formally shake my hand, but mine was the only one he shook. I remained with the others at the ship's rail till the canoe disappeared. The Captain locked himself in his cabin until the following day when he once again became the impersonal, cold ship's captain, as if Button had never existed. We were the last white men to see him for a very long time.

Fifteen years after that last afternoon, while in London, I learned that other whites had looked for him without success. The missionary Allen Gardiner, "the fanatic shepherd of souls lost in God's forgotten climes," who counted on Button for his missionary undertaking, was shipwrecked and met an end reserved for many in the southern waters. Sheltered in caves along the coast, Gardiner and three other survivors resisted for a time, hoping to be rescued, but the southern winter caught them while the floating fires and the dark silhouettes surrounded them. They starved to death, frozen in those caverns, but not before the missionary had left behind a diary written almost until the day he died.

This was, in a sense, the beginning of the end. Gardiner,

as martyr, inspired the founding of the Mission, but what is hard to believe—and yet that's how it was—is that the Mission was founded in London, twenty thousand miles from the Cape, with Button in mind as its future foundation stone. Then other missionaries came, once again insistently looking for him so that he could become what England had trained him to be: a bridge between Great Britain and his people, an interpreter of the goodwill of white men come from the east.

On the grey morning in June when we buried my mother, Mallory had put on his uniform and was quiet and somber, almost without glancing at me. There were three of us: my father, myself, and a Catholic priest he had sent someone at full gallop to fetch the night of her last agony and who had been pulled out of bed with practically nothing on. The man must have donned his religious habit while on top of his horse, so irrevocable and urgent had been the order given by Mallory to the peon in broken Spanish: "Bring the priest any way you can or else I'll go get him myself." In addition there were the well-known silver coins that I shall bring up later.

We stood motionless beside the open grave on the plain. A dismal drizzle was falling with the same desolation as I saw it falling on the ocean later on. The priest finished his prayers, threw me a compassionate look, shook Mallory's hand, mounted his horse, and left. It was all over. On our return home, my father was silent for a long time at the window, watching the drizzle as if unyielding fatigue had overwhelmed him. Then he removed his jacket, pulled on his poncho, stirred the fire, and finally, as if everything before had only been done in preparation, he grabbed his bottle and a glass.

Two days later, after hoarsely clearing his throat several times, he seemed to come back to life. He took his boots down from the bed and sat staring at the floor, breathing heavily. He slowly raised his head and watched me. It was the first time in ages that my father was actually *seeing* me. It was a long, silent, and mutual recognition. He struggled to his feet and rested his enormous hands on my shoulders. To me, he looked like the Devil himself and he smelled bad, but I didn't move. Then he said:

"Do you want to know what the sea is like?"

I didn't dare answer because I never could tell why or what he had in mind when he said or did things. He pulled me up off the bed and pushed me to the door. We walked awhile and he stopped. With his outstretched arm he traced a circle that took in the horizon.

"The sea is like that," he said, "like this endless, monotonous land, but it is all water. The house is like a ship."

That night he emptied a pitcher of water on the back of his neck all at once, shook his head like a horse breathing hard, and with his fingers pushed back his long blond hair.

"It's time you learned something," he said.

He lit the oil lamp, and with his arm he swept away several days' crumbs as well as some utensils in his way on the table and set the light down in the centre of the heavy planks. I had eaten nothing but stale biscuits for two days but it dawned on me that his thoughts weren't on food. The shadows cast by the lamp and the recent loss of my mother made me regard him almost with terror. The poncho he was wearing like a gaucho made him more imposing. His boots were still the same old high black army boots. He had never mistreated me, but he had ignored me for such a long time that I didn't trust him. The words "madman" and "heretic" which I had been hearing since I reached the age of reason came to mind, and I wondered if the meaning behind them wasn't even more sinister than the one I gave them. He went over to the shelf where he treasured what was left of his identity or his past and took something out. He returned to the table and set a book down under the light, in front of me.

"It's time you learned how to read," he said.

I was looking at a book for the first time. Perhaps during

all those years, Mallory had read while I was sleeping or maybe I had watched him but was too little to understand what he was doing.

He started to turn the first pages with a care I had never seen in him before. In a thick voice, he said:

"This book talks about the sea."

That evening I entered a current, and I knew it would never end; it would carry me along in its flow to my death and would be the only company and dependable refuge I would ever be given a chance to know. A few months later I was able to read for him— in a loud, halting voice—whole sections of that book which told the story of a man born in the city of York, who was shipwrecked in seas far from home for an Englishman but near this country.

One day my father disappeared, leaving me alone at home. When he came back, without saying a word he spilled five or six books onto the table, some of them in Spanish. I discovered that this ambiguous gesture had something to do with his memory of my mother. As if also teaching me to read and write in Spanish would have been both a betrayal of him and an act of love for her.


William Scott Mallory had come from the Cape of Good Hope and before that from Cape Verde, and, before that, from a port called Liverpool where he had shipped out, and, even before that, from the London suburb where he was born. Who could have imagined that I, his South American son, born in the remote plains of the southern part of the world, would return years later to London under such strange circumstances?

Be that as it may, in June of 1806 my father had disembarked from the *Encounter* in Quilmes—under Beresford's command—near the anchorage in the harbor of Barragán, had gone off to Buenos Aires in what he recalled as harsh and torrential rain, and had fought in the city's muddy streets.

In Mallory's version, the explanation for the English defeat mixed reproaches to his superiors and accusations of erroneous political machinations with the surprise resistance from a plaza that, behind a semblance of deceptive calm, had fiercely defended itself all alone. They had been promised glory and easy spoils. Neither of these two came to fruition but my father had acquired a good number of silver coins, wisely distributed in the beginning among only a few, and which later made it possible for him to settle down in Lobos.

My father had been an invader but he did not shun his duties to the country which finally ended up adopting him. In 1823, after a bloody raid by the Pampa's Indians, the militia came to Lobos to recruit people for a large expedition to punish the Indians and drive them from the frontier, farther south of Tandil. My mother had died a year before. Mallory had stayed sober since then and perhaps for him joining up was an act of desperation or of evading for a time the fatherly duties which he had assumed but were now a burden or a bore. In any case, he offered himself as neighbor and volunteer. There was one obstacle. Mallory was going off to fight the Indians in his English uniform.

"You can't go this way," Captain Conell, who was in charge of the recruits, had said to him.

My father didn't understand.

"You can't go this way, dressed like the English," Conell repeated, no doubt uncomfortable because all he needed were men, even if they were naked, but a military blind spot made him reject the uniform of the former invaders.

My father looked himself over from his boots up.

"Like this, or else I don't go," he said.

The faces in the patrol studied him from their horses. No one knew what decision to make. Another neighbor resolved the conflict.

"The gringo is a good fighter, let him wear a poncho on top."

That's how Mallory set out to fight the Indians.

What was simply the natural chain of events still seems strange, or perhaps it only seems strange to me. I can't help thinking that my father's coming to Buenos Aires and, in consequence, my birth had their origin in the letter the ambitious Riggs Pophan sent from the city on the Cape to the influential Lord Castlereagh, future Minister of Foreign Relations, in London, *"I consider the possession of a colony on the coasts of South America to be full of incalculable advantages... ";* or that the suggestion to invade Buenos Aires should be accepted—with its fatal results for England on a military level—and that many years later Lord Castlereagh should commit suicide because of political pressures added to a certain mental imbalance, slashing his throat with his own razor; and that the man was direct uncle to the Captain, who years later came south on a scientific as well as strategic mission; and finally that I, John William Guevara—offspring of the encounter of that soldier of a failed expedition and a woman of this country—should happen to meet the Captain, sail with him, and find out now about his death by his own hand, with his own razor, just like his uncle, Lord Castlereagh.

If I believed in fate and the gods, I might believe that this weave of causes and effects forms a sequence where I fit perfectly and in which this request of yours, Mr. MacDowell or MacDowness, makes sense: to justify a story in which failures are turned around to condemn Button and at the same time rehabilitate the Captain, thus closing a kind of circle. Have I gone mad? No doubt I have. But England has hardly ever cared disinterestedly about the world existing behind the facts. And what I have ended up being interested in is precisely that: what was behind the facts.

A week has gone by since my last entry. I woke up before daybreak, upset by a nightmare. I had qualms about rousing Graciana, and I let her sleep. I lit the stove and heated water for the maté, waiting for the pale glow on the horizon to become daylight. For a man my age to tell a dream may seem inappropriate, but I didn't dream of myself as a man but as the child I had been; from there, memory brought to the surface of sleep the terror of seeing a savage for the first time.

One afternoon, I must have been eight years old then, I had galloped to the lagoon. Lying on my stomach on the ground, next to some weeds, I was on the lookout for an otter when the unmistakable sound of horses trotting on loose clay made me jump to my feet. They were three, two of them with their long bamboo spears at the ready; a headband held together the other's mop of coarse hair. I recall myself being looked over by those dark flat faces. Frozen with fear, I watched an arm raised to point me out, and I heard a high-pitched gibberish I couldn't understand. An interminable moment went by, they finally turned around their horses were loaded down with bundles of skins—and went away. They were the ones whom white men called friendly Indians, who came to trade at the general store, but no one had yet told me this. Later on I heard it: what had attracted their attention was my yellow hair.

That was the memory revived in the dream, together with the naked bodies of the Yámanas and the cold wind of Cape Horn. A fire they would light again night after night—with the atavistic desire to penetrate fear as well as the darkness— and which to us men on deck looked taller and taller, more and more impressive. Bent over, a figure goes up to it and feeds it, and then another and yet another. Women, children, and dogs packed close together, on their haunches around the flames that rose, as if by magic, from between their fingers in spite of the rain and the soaked branches. Absorbed in their work, without letting out a sound, as if their lives and their souls depended on the fire's staying alive. Eyes reddened by smoke were proof of this adoration. Something I can't describe, for which I can find no name, stirred inside me. A sorrow as heavy as a rock which seemed to come from the beginning of time and made me seek with my eyes the Captain or one of my comrades, in whose glance I discovered the same indefinable uneasiness. And then, those beings would climb into their canoes where the fire was kept alive in small embers, and they would paddle furtively, gliding around our ship, describing circles, so that in the dark the light of the eternal fire seemed to rise out of the water and perform a menacing dance, again and again, until dawn.

On deck, shivering with cold, the boy I was then paced from port to starboard, unable to take his eyes from the illumined bodies. The word *cannibals* pronounced by the men who had left the ship to look for the stolen whaleboat made me shake even more.

Have you ever been face to face with what the books call a *savage*, a naked man with ribs exposed, covered with grease, his genitals swollen with disease, his face painted with white streaks, and tangled, coarse hair? It was hard to discover the man in that being in whose character was manifest a creature full of trust that in the next minute could be overcome by blind, irrational fury. Have you, Mr. MacDowell or MacDowness, ever seen that strange being leap across the ages and appear before you in the helpless state of the origin of our species, a man like you and me who reproduces, eats, and dies like you, invents gods, hunts, goes to war, domesticates dogs, and starts a fire? Once you have seen him you never forget him.

That is how I met Button, but it was through him that, behind such an appearance, I discovered the man I believed did not exist. And behind the man, a people with beliefs and spirit, with respect for life in all its forms, whom I had not known before and would not know again.

In a little while it will be daybreak; I can feel the cool of night that comes before dawn. Ajax is asleep under my table. When the sun comes up, I'll put on the poncho that was my father's and go out into the countryside. On horseback the curlicues and deliriums of the written word are put out of mind and the primordial link with the world is restored, something it is best not to forget.

I recall something in Mallory that resembled laughter. It would come up in the reading or writing sessions he provided whenever he was ready, that is, at dawn or at noon but always with the same zeal or even challenge. What I learned during those hours included anything from a ship's mast and rigging to Ben Jonson's poems. He seemed to consider it a heritage that, in turn, had been left to him by someone about whom he never spoke. He would say he was passing on to me something worth more than money and that he wanted to leave it to me so that, among uncivilized persons, like him I might enjoy its benefits. Surely you can understand, Mr. MacDowell or MacDowness, what this signifies on the lips of an Englishman.

Above all he spoke with special pleasure about London's taverns. I imagine it was not only because one drank by the bottle there, as I was able to confirm years later, but also because business deals and voyages might come up around those greasy tables. Without forgetting the rooms upstairs in the taverns. It was in one of those squalid places that he received on one shoulder the shot he liked to pass off before gullible persons as a war wound. It's apropos to mention that my father doesn't seem to have been very fastidious in his choice of women.

"If you want a woman, go after her. If you have to share her, share her."

Before my astonished eyes, at such times he would open his mouth and let out a powerful, hoarse, drawn-out laugh. And all at once the dogs under the table would take sudden fright and begin to whine and bark into the air, joining his laughter in a wild fit of restlessness. A black one, his favorite, would raise his snout and, rolling his eyes, would hurl a doleful lament into the air.

As a matter of fact, in English he had said "a female." I was twelve and didn't know much about females except in reference to animal couplings in the country. However, Mallory failed to notice certain details. Going all the way with his theory about women is how he came to enjoy the dubious prestige of that scar. In effect, during those years back in London, he shared the mistress of a cooper who was unaware of the broad-minded habits of his rival, especially since he did not know that he had one. The barrel-maker was a married man and perhaps he would not have minded his own wife's cuckolding him, but that his mistress, whose keep at the tavern he paid, should deceive him was something else. Mallory used to lie in ambush under the landing on the second floor, waiting for the cooper to leave the bedsheets free. Since the man had to leave at a prudent hour, my father could enjoy his lady and a previously warmed bed until late the next morning. While lying in wait for the cooper's departure one night, he had the urge to urinate and this was increased by his squatting position and the gin he had imbibed. He left his hideout stealthily, went to the railing, and there did what he had to do. The tavern owner was the one who received the downpour. He rushed upstairs and jumped on my father, intending to beat him up. But my father was not a small man. Hearing the ruckus, the barrel-maker came out and, without stopping to think, the owner called him a cuckold. The man drew a gun and fired at the shape he saw. He hit my father's shoulder. Amidst the shouts of those who had gotten out of bed and those who had not yet left the place, William Scott Mallory of the British Royal Navy was carried bodily to an apothecary, whom, judging by the way he sewed up the wound, they must have found asleep.

The only times I heard Mallory laugh were during those crazy lessons. Fascinated by the dogs' behavior, I often planned to bring up the subject of women in order to set off the off-key concert under the table. But I never did.

On some days he was in a terrible humor. At the slightest distraction on my part, he would drill right through me with ice-cold eyes between blood-red lids. I had mistaken a schooner for a cutter. He banged on the table with his open palm.

"No, *carajo!*" he shouted in Spanish.

To this, the dogs hardly bothered to pay the slightest attention.

William Scott Mallory had survived twenty years at sea. He could not stand the endless pampa for that long. He grew impenetrable and limited himself to his relationship with his faithful dogs. When I reached my seventeenth year, he hanged himself.

The Captain slashing his throat in front of the mirror; my father hanging from a crossbeam in a farmhouse at the farthest reaches of the world. He had on the uniform in which he had come to the Viceroyalty of the River Plate almost twenty years before. Mallory had trusted no one: a slip of paper stuck out from between the buttons on his jacket. In his handwriting it read: *William Scott Mallory, may he rest in peace.* I imagine that in the last moments, before he passed the rope around the beam, before tying the knot, perhaps while writing his own name on the paper, he felt as never before that he was in a remote foreign place, where he seemed to have come only to father a son who at the last moment he also felt was an alien and a stranger to him. He did not trust anyone. Perhaps his final thoughts were for my mother or for the London suburb where he had been born or for the sea which was in his blood. All I can say is that I crossed his hands on his chest and closed his eyes. I folded the slip of paper and stuck it into one of his pockets.

What I know for sure is that Mallory cured himself of his perpetual drinking to educate me and that once this was accomplished there was nothing else for him to do. As his only legacy or as a premonitory sign of what is happening right now, on his table he left the books, the candle, pen and ink. It was the only sign he left me, in case I should want to interpret it. This and the documents in which he certified that this house and this piece of land were now mine.

With his death, I was now all alone and had to go out in search of my own livelihood.

# FOLIO THREE

Nothing was keeping me in the country except two graves swept by the wind. The plain saw Mallory and me off with a storm; a violent wind from the pampas blew all one day and all one night. Then the sky grew clear again and the heat returned. Following an obscure mandate I can only ascribe to the influence of my mother in my childhood, I decided to place my trust in the Church and, in case I should some day return, I left the deed to my father's property in the modest ranch house which served as chapel in Lobos. An old mulata, who had always been with my mother, remained at the house with the dogs.

I remember the day before my departure. I looked sadly at every object, every tree, every bird. Bitter sorrow, in which hopelessness and being orphaned joined forces, was eating my heart. That night I threw my saddlebags, with the few possessions I was taking along, across my horse's back and left.

On a high clear morning I saw what I believed was the sea. Only later did I learn that that enormous expanse of water was the River Plate. I sat down on the bluff before its quiet waters, listening to the screech of the seagulls, wishing to feel that the *Encounter* had one day come that way. Following the riverbank, I entered Buenos Aires on its south side and asked for the Hotel de Faunch, which Mallory had mentioned to me several times. I didn't want to look up the home of the Guevara family. My mother's memory was perfect, and I would have completely rejected any information about her prior to my birth.

This was only a half-truth, Mr. MacDowell or Mac-Downess; the boy I was at the time did not dare come out with the whole truth. The Guevaras, my grandparents, were gentry in Buenos Aires, and instinct told me that they would not have welcomed the bastard's visit.

The cries of the street vendors, houses with large potbellied window grilles, and a few women I saw behind those grilles or whom I passed in the street make up my first memory of a city. At one corner a fat negress said to me:

"Buy a cake, gentleman."

I bought it from her. The gentleman part impressed me.

That evening in the dining room of the Hotel de Faunch people talked with natural and elegant gestures I had never seen before. I seemed to understand that it was all about important matters, the clues to a circle whose secret I would never be able to discover. The women, above all, were disturbing. I could not take my eyes off the smooth necks and shoulders, their bosoms openly exposed. That they should speak with such ease to the men amazed and disturbed me. Today I can't help laughing at that boy whom everyone in the place regarded with side glances, half mocking or half pitying. At some point I noticed this. The blood rushed to my face: I was an ignoramus, a country bumpkin, and, despite the color of my hair, no more than a gaucho. I was boiling over with rage, with the need to show them that I was a man and not a boy, that I knew how to break in horses and race them over the pampa like an arrow, that I had read books they didn't even know about and spoke English. I left the table and went to bed without eating.

The next day, somewhat out of sorts, distracted, I walked aimlessly around town until I came to the esplanade of the Fort. No important ships were to be seen on the river. At least not the one I had imagined would be mine. That very morning I sold my horse to the hotel's proprietor and asked him how and where I could get a ship. He gave me the names of two ships riding at anchor in the port of Montevideo. A strong gale several weeks before had caused them serious damage, and they were in for repairs. All I had to do was cross the river and see what there was for me.

Crossing the mighty river was my first sailing experience and I would be lying if I said I liked it.

Reaching the small schooner in a battered cart whose rotting boards were falling apart and the mocking help of the dock workers who at the cry of "There goes another one!" heaved us by the seat of the pants so we could make it over the side of a small river boat, was my first *taste of the sea.* Boarding rather ignobly like that was very different from the scenes of taut sails, fair wind, and precise orders with which I had embellished my first passage. I had paid the cheapest fare and had only the right to remain on deck, crammed together with several other wretches traveling under the same conditions. The River Plate is not the Thames, Mr. Mac-Dowell or MacDowness: it was nine endless hours on a choppy river. According to the pilot, with a straight face before my wild-eyed look, it had been an excellent crossing.

I liked Montevideo better than Buenos Aires. Better sheltered, its natural harbor was without doubt more important, and several ships flying different flags accounted for considerable activity. In this city's air I perceived modesty and at the same time an activity and a dynamism that appealed to me on my first sally into the world. Of all the ships anchored in the port, one seemed majestic to me. I stared at it for a long while, trying to match what I saw with the names of the rigging Mallory had taught me. When nightfall carried the day's stifling heat upriver, I experienced a feeling of well-being that little by little expanded into a happiness I hadn't known until then. I was beginning to feel free, the master of my own actions and my destiny. I no longer had to account to anyone and was ready for anything that came my way. When the ships lit their lamps, I had recovered my appetite. I went into an inn and ate fried fish, which turned out to be the most delicious dish I had ever tasted in my life and, to go with it, I drank a pitcher of wine. Seeing my father in his cups, I had often vowed that I would never touch alcohol, but this promise quickly vanished along with remorse. I could hardly rise from the table. With my arms around my saddlebags I fell asleep like a log among the bundles and ropes in the storeroom at the rear.

When I awoke, the night was pitch black. The ships in the river could no longer be made out, and I could hardly see the lights on the masts rocking in the moonless dark, but it was enough to make me experience an anxiety that linked me to those ships in a way that not even I could wholly understand. I went back into the inn. There was a group of men at a table away from the others. Large candles and a lamp heightened the color of their faces and their clothes; I knew it was what I was looking for. There was no doubting it, men of the sea. I recognized them by their weather-beaten skin and certain indefinable traces which immediately brought Mallory to mind. They were not just any seamen, and their ship could not be just any ship. One in particular drew my notice: he was eating, upright in his chair, his back straight as a board, transmitting a sensation of pride and assurance that made him eclipse the others, including me. Unaware of it, I gradually drew closer to that table like an insect to the light, but not only because of what I saw but what I could hear. The rumble of words was making sense in the midst of the laughter behind the words, forming phrases that intimately threaded their way into my ear. They were speaking in English.

I had come to within two steps of the table and stayed there, apparently with a stupid air, when the man with a back as straight as a board turned his head to look at me. The others watched me too. Word for word, the man said in a low voice: "We have a guest." I was speechless. One of them said in broken Spanish that amused the others:

"What's the matter, boy? Have you lost something here?"

I moved closer.

"I'm looking for work on board," I managed to say. "I want to ship out," I said in English with my heart going full gallop.

The surprise was now theirs.

"The boy speaks good English," the one straight as a board said. Then he asked me if I had come off some American ship.

"No," I found myself saying, "I'm Argentine, I come from Buenos Aires."

"Well, I'll be—," the man said.

I took this important man to be none less than the captain of one of the ships, I should have guessed it from the first. The rest was like a dream. They sat me at their table, discovered that my father had been English and my mother Creole, and that I was an orphan. They invited me to eat, for which I thanked them, accepting only a glass of wine. One said that it was quite convenient for the ship, and for the mission as well, to count on a cabin boy who spoke both Spanish and English. The man with the proud bearing concluded that I would ship out with them that very night. The ship was ready; they had finished the repairs and were weighing anchor at daybreak.

"You're going to scrub and scrape and caulk with tar until your arms drop off, boy. You will learn very fast what a ship of His British Majesty is."

I almost did something stupid: jump to my feet and vigorously shake his hand, promising to do all that and much more without batting an eye; I had a hard time staying in my chair. They proposed a toast and we clinked glasses.

"Were you ever on a real ship, son?" The captain finally asked—cutting short the emotions stirring in me—, staring at me with eyes that pierced my face like nails.

I stammered out the things Mallory had told me about his sea voyages and started to get all tangled up in a pathetically clumsy way.

"Sir, this fellow can't tell the difference between the crow's nest and the cathead," someone said.

The captain smiled but kept staring at me. He asked my name.

"Why Guevara?" He wanted to know. "Why Guevara and not Mallory, boy?"

The others looked at me, amused and curious.

I shrugged to hide my embarrassment and blurted out: "Not Mallory. Guevara."

Later, amid the river's darkness, the sound of oars cutting the water, and the chant of the men keeping the beat, I experienced for the first time the feeling of brotherhood, difficult to explain, which for the man of the sea is the most precious, the closest thing to what on land we call home. I felt that I was part of a ship's crew. The euphoria of this feeling made me lose my shyness, and I asked:

"Captain, what is the ship's course?"

"Captain?" The laughter all around left me open-mouthed. "I'm not the captain, Jack. I'm your boatswain."

Then he said:

"We're on our way to Tierra del Fuego, boy. To Patagonia. To the south, to hell itself, to the asshole of the world. And there is your ship, the *Beagle*. Two hundred and forty tons, eight meters of beam, thirty-three long, and a crew of seventy-four. What do you think of it?"

The ship appeared between the water and the night, outlined by the lights on board. The river's waves broke with a soft splash against the huge creaking hulk, enormous as the round belly of a benign mythological animal, as I like to remember it now. When they let down the ladder, something was released inside me like a taut rope: a wild sense of joy. I couldn't believe it had all happened like this, so easily. I had to fling my saddlebags over my shoulder and hold on to the dinghy's wooden seat with all my strength so as not to jump out with a yell and have them believe I had gone crazy. I had no idea why they were laughing, perhaps at me, but I joined the general merriment with roars of laughter.

Once I was aboard, my euphoria disappeared. Overwhelmed by a sense of almost religious reverence, I was rooted to the spot, contemplating the outsized rigging gently swayed by the river and listening to the ripple of the wind in the sails, the creaking of the wooden masts, music that from now on would be one of the familiar sounds in my life, so much so that with the years I couldn't fall asleep without hearing it.

The boatswain told me:

"I'll be right back. Stay right here."

I gazed at the stars shining, protective and remote in the moonless dark, beyond the feeble lantern on the main mast. I turned my face to the lights ashore like someone looking at a place no longer his, already in the past. At last, from the hatchway the boatswain made signs for me to come. We went down and I followed him along a narrow, low, winding passage. We stopped before a door, and my guide knocked softly.

When the door opened, what appeared before me was a cabin crammed with books, maps, unidentifiable objects which I learned afterwards were instruments for marine and astronomical calibrations. Two pictures recaptured a country-side where men and women were riding horses, surrounded by innumerable dogs, a countryside that was nothing like the one I had just left. The cabin gave off a strong smell of tobacco. The impression was intense but vanished as soon as the man who had been over on one side, with his back to me, appeared in front of us. I knew now why the sailors in the boat had laughed at my confusion. Anyone seeing the man who stood before me now would know at once that he and no other was in command of that ship.

Much later, I learned that the Empire had slipped into this cabin its most valuable attributes and purest values and that the man who appeared under the small lamps affixed to the dark wood of the walls was a privileged specimen of what England had come to represent.

Your letter arrived one month ago today. We are in November, and spring displays its undeniable and quiet beauty on the prairie. I know its contents by heart but I reread it. Mr. MacDowell or MacDowness, why do I have the feeling that it conceals a threat? Its effect on me belongs to the order of the unfamiliar. All at once I recall Japan's interior sea, its treacherous green depth, where we were detained once by the threat of a case of scurvy on board ship. Lying flat on deck in the paralyzing heat, we talked with the oyster fishermen. One of them showed us a pearl. In the rough dark palm of his hand it shone like a tiny translucent planet. He picked up an oyster and explained to us drowsy sailors how the miracle took place: a parasite or a grain of sand works its way into the valve. The oyster defends itself from that foreign body by patiently wrapping it with its filament of nacre to immobilize it, and the result is a unique object. The oyster's instinct, like any animal's, is to protect itself, except that its defense produces a pearl.

The letter has affected me like a strange organism from which I defend myself by wrapping it in the endless thread of this story intended for no one. And over and above that, may I consider this story "my pearl"? The strange activity I've rushed into makes me ask whether sometimes words don't lead us to folly.

More simply put, the fact is that the story I'm about to tell embarrasses me. I realize that perhaps it's easier to maneuver a ship than to put the past into words.

As antidote, these last few days I've dedicated myself to domestic tasks, to my horses or going to the general store where I inquire for news from Buenos Aires. Resigning herself to my new activity, Graciana goes on looking suspiciously at these papers that have an extraordinary attraction for her. Her gentleness calms me, and her body, so young and generous, tears me away from my loneliness. Her being here establishes the counterbalance I need, after all, to be able to go on. I am coming to the point in this story where I meet Button. What I've been through weighs heavily on me and at times it all seems like a dream.

What I have written above is now two days old. I've felt a curious reluctance to go on, and I spent the last part of the afternoon riding to the lagoon on horseback. There I always come to a ford where the tracks of the Indians persist in the hard ground. Once, as a boy, I saw a herd of cattle that some gauchos were bringing from the frontier, stray cattle rustled by Pampa Indians and recovered many leagues to the south, beyond the Colorado river. They said there were about thirty thousand. I remember how the ground trembled, as I clung to my mother's skirt. Years later, before going to London, I imagined something similar in its populace, such was the size of that unknown city, constantly mentioned by sailors on board ship.

Insects circle the oil lamp. At night the prairie is like an unmoving sea. Night takes over the world, and sometimes one has to murmur, to say something. The prairie swallows everything. And then one has to murmur, as if to make sure he's alive.

The Captain. As time went on I understood why those who sailed with him blindly entrusted their lives to him and why they also obeyed him blindly. That night his ice-blue eyes observed me without any discernible expression. He was a young man with a sturdy build, energetic and self-controlled, with a character whose firmness quickly turned to inflexibility. He brooked no discussion, much less disobedience, from his men in matters of navigation. For me, Robert FitzRoy, aristocratic and proud, descendant of an illegitimate son of Charles II, grandson of the Duke of Grafton, and nephew of Lord Castlereagh, Marquis of Londonderry, was always simply the Captain. As a seaman, he was one of the most expert I have ever known. His self-assurance, derived from his scientific training—he could predict the approach of a storm with an instrument he himself had devised—was transmitted to the crew. In his cabin, at meals, and in his treatment of others, he maintained the same discretion and good breeding he would show at the most fashionable dinner in London. He was inflexible and obsessively demanding when it came to his work.

This was the man I met face to face that evening, surrounded, almost consecrated, in my innocent eyes by all the symbols that helped to bring out his gifts as a privileged son of England.

I am a fifty-three-year-old man remembering a seventeen-year-old youth, and in spite of my reluctance, Mr. MacDowell or MacDowness, I can't prevent a distant flicker of emotions I thought were lost from creeping into this story.

I see myself one morning, next to the wheel. On the port side, dawn is merely a pale glow on the horizon, and to starboard far away, above a blue and green strip of sea, the dark outline of the high Patagonian cliffs is just beginning to sketch itself. I stare amazed at enormous patches on the water which a sudden jet betrays as a school of whales. Shaking with fear, I measure the smallness of the ship that is sort of tiptoeing its way through the midst of those tame monsters. I see myself in the kitchen peeling potatoes, sleepily repeating the names of the rigging, scrubbing the deck with cracked red hands, failing to carry out orders correctly, regularly passing the tests which every beginner is put through. But most of all I watch the foam on the prow, I listen to the waves against planking, the icy south wind cuts my face, I am seventeen years old, and I have the universal sensation of being alive.

My first unforgettable storm at sea comes back to me.

We have left behind the Cape Virgin islands and are heading for the strait of Le Maire. It is past noon. Like a warning sign, an albatross plays with the wind, letting itself be borne by the currents which the storm is forming overhead and which here below torment the ship and the crew. The groundswell increases and the day grows dark. The waves follow one another short and fast; the ship's prow noses through the water. Before we finish hauling down sails, the now enormous combers crash against the hull and sweep the deck from end to end. The water hits me with great force and in a second I'm soaked through to the bone; clinging to the gunwale, I don't know what saint to commend myself to. Day has turned into night and the storm is upon us, gripping the ship which, at the mercy of the sea, protests with tremendous groans. With a sudden cramp in my stomach, I become thoroughly aware of my insignificance and—what until yesterday seemed inconceivable—of the ship's fragility. I manage to respond like an automaton to the instructions of the pilot who has called me to his side and who, shouting and swearing in something like a fit of madness, displays rabid joy. The Captain remains on the bridge, calmly giving precise, rapid orders which the men interpret immediately and carry out without hesitation. Giant waves whose existence I had never imagined carry us to lofty peaks and then dash us down to the depths. I don't know where the sky and the earth are; everything is wind, water and darkness.

When the storm subsides, I realize within a kind of stupor that hours have gone by. Fourteen hours, I was told afterwards. Storm clouds race at top speed across the sky, letting us glimpse a distant, cold and brilliant moon. At daybreak I go down to the bunks to drink a mug of hot coffee and remove my clothes. The pilot slaps me on the back and says:

"Well done, boy."

I take care to look out of the corner of my eye at my companions' weather-beaten faces, expecting to be ridiculed, but nothing happens. What does follow is a hellish fatigue, all my bones ache and my hands are raw. I fall into my bunk and sink into a profound, unbroken sleep. Days later the pilot sends for me. He presents me with a pipe, the first I ever owned; I still keep it as a lucky charm.

I had begun to understand something of the aura surrounding the place we were heading for. I had been born in the Confederation but I had never heard of those places that English seamen spoke about so knowingly, and yet they were in the southern part of a land that was my country.

My baptism at sea, Mr. MacDowell or MacDowness, occurred in the labyrinth of islands most feared by the ships of the whole world: Cape Horn. This liquid hell was surrounded by a dismal fascination with ships that never returned; shipwrecked sailors who left signals on rocks or a bottle buried in the sand; living cadavers who took refuge in caves along the coast around whose mortal remains hovered another motive for fright: the terrifying winter of Cape Horn.

Only the long familiarity of years with that place of mild summers and supernatural peace was able to change that first impression.

Nothing but the germ of madness inherent in the human race justifies the fact that men rush off to sea. Once you get the taste of it, it's impossible to retreat. The sea is an excess, and as such it involves a certain amount of wisdom. Although I never believed it, somehow I must have been a typical man of the sea who chose this land to retire to as another kind of excess. I chose my mother's language, and these plains will receive me some day like my mother's bosom.

I have a large number of maps in my trunk; they've always fascinated me. An enormous portion of Patagonian territory appears on those old maps under the name *res nullius*, no-man's land. It's my country. Have you ever been in Patagonia, Mr. MacDowell or MacDowness? Can you even imagine it? Can you imagine a colossal corridor of winds whose floor is a plateau which descends from the mountains toward the east and leans out over the sea in gigantic concave cliffs? Can you imagine a horse and its rider going at full speed, fascinated by the stationary presence of a giant rock-like cloud out of Genesis, which hangs motionless in a crystal-clear sky at noon, and the rider racing for the simple pleasure of passing under the motionless cloud? Can you imagine an immensity which could hold a thousand Londons?

And one morning we were there at the end of the world, in front of those steep rugged rocks and gloomy islands and, farther below, nothing. Next to the Captain at the ship's rail I took in everything, discovering a very old world which seemed only recently created. The Captain pointed out an island.

"The Horn itself," he said. "It needs no description, it's not easy to confuse."

A black rock projected from the water; islets of ice drifted offshore. The Captain seemed to be as comfortable and satisfied as in his garden at home. He asked me to bring him a mug of coffee in his cabin.

In those two months he had taken a certain liking to me. He was a man of culture and he appreciated any example of this—which could only rarely be offered him on the high seas—as a special treat. At his request, I had explained how Mallory had made me read some English and world classics. This drew from him a curious comment in which racial pride mingled with the simple acknowledgment of a fact:

"England is everywhere."

I had never thought of it in this way, but when he said it I realized that it was not far from the truth.

However, I should no doubt explain something, Mr.

MacDowell or MacDowness. There was admiration but there was nothing filial in my feeling for the Captain and I dare say no man who ever sailed with him could have harbored such a feeling. He created a vacuum around him. He was dry and aloof, with something obsessive about his need to exert control over others, which became painfully obvious in the case of Button and of which I would be the principal witness in the years that followed. Not that he was a bad man, but he definitely disliked any kind of proximity to others or any theme other than God, the sea, or nautical science.

Something comes to mind that is nothing but an example of the Captain's character and perhaps, by extension, of the general character with which England imposed its rules: the word *Tekeenica,* used by the Captain to name the country of Button and his people. In reality, as I learned from Button himself, that sound literally signifies "I don't understand what you say," which is what the Yámanas would answer the Captain:

*"Teke uneka."*

But as they repeated it constantly, he deduced before long that they were saying the name of their country, and that's the name he gave it.


It had been months since I first shipped out, and I could almost call myself a man of the sea. We had gone up the coast of Chile and returned to the southern islands where we were riding at anchor, taking readings for a survey ordered by the Captain. In a way, I had grown used to those shadows that glided silently around the ship in their canoes and lit huge fires along the coast, perforating the darkness of night. From the ship's rail, I could not take my eyes off those bodies or the fires. I didn't believe they were actually cannibals—as my companions said—but they could indeed seem so around the fire's glow. Tall flames releasing red tongues in the middle of the blackness, in the middle of a night without moon or stars. A fire that breathed and rose higher and higher, between thick puffs of smoke. We often saw them follow the ship's course, racing along the coast. And yet I had never run into a single one of them.

One afternoon the group of men taking hydrographic measurements came back to the ship with the news that the savages had stolen one of the whaleboats. The Captain selected search parties to go find it. I went in one of those groups. We came up with nothing. Once they stole something, we never saw it again. Not a single trace, no sign of it. They simply disappeared before our eyes. Half an hour later we would see them racing over the rocks to let us think they were not the same ones. The same thing for days or weeks.

Winter was upon us; in a last effort to recover the boat, furious, the Captain brought hostages aboard. There were three of them, and their names and ages corresponded to the places or circumstances in which they had been found and also to imagination: little Fuegia, a girl nine or ten years old; York Minster, more than twenty, strong and mistrustful; and Boat Memory, younger and reserved. A few days later, the Captain himself went ashore to carry on the search, and his boat was on its way back to the ship when it was surrounded by ten or fifteen canoes packed with Yámanas. In one that was near the Captain's long boat there was a boy fifteen or sixteen, on his feet. The angry Captain made up his mind to take another hostage to frighten the Indians. He seized the boy roughly by the arm. In the same movement, the boy jumped into the boat to keep his own canoe—where a voice, perhaps his father's, cried out—from capsizing. The Captain tore some buttons from his overcoat and threw them into the canoe as a form of payment. A great commotion followed, and the incident might have turned dangerous. On deck, a seaman fired a shot into the air. At last, we succeeded in hauling up the boats. The last hostage was baptized Jemmy Button as a reminder of the price paid for him.

I stopped writing and made an effort to remember. I tried to go deep into the past to see whether in that first encounter with Button there had been anything, any sign of the importance that the boy, converted into a man, would have years later in my life and in future events. There is nothing, Mr. MacDowell or MacDowness. Memory shuffles Button and all his countrymen into a common picture of strange beings coming from the beginning of time, for whom I felt both rejection and pity, while trying to take in the naked state of the women in the canoes.

The Captain made them wash themselves and put on clothes. They were not displeased with us: dazzled by all the new things before their eyes, in a few days they moved about the ship with natural ease. They learned English at a staggering pace. They possessed a mimetic gift; they copied language the way one copies gestures, attitudes, or skills needed to survive. The first thing the Captain taught Button was *You may call me Jemmy Button,* and he repeated it, cheerfully pacing the deck. He stopped in front of me and repeated for the hundredth time: *You may call me Jemmy Button.* I looked at him and touched his chest with my index finger:

"Jemmy Button."

I touched mine and said:

"Jack."

His face lit up. He understood that the name the whites had given him was just Jemmy Button and not "You may call me Jemmy Button." To my surprise, immediately touching his chest with his thumb, he said:

"Jemmy Button, Yámana," and pointing to my chest, "Jack, white."

It was the first time we communicated and how I learned his people's name.

Button was the most intelligent, the one most inclined to learn about the things that intrigued him and the most anxious to let me see his country. He made signs to let me know that he would show it to me. He was so talented a mimic that often a long time would go by in which, thanks to that gift of his, we understood each other perfectly without need for words.

Several days after the Yámanas came aboard, the Captain called me to his cabin and told me he wanted me to do something important. He had decided to take the natives to London and wanted me to stay close to them, especially to Button, since we were almost the same age. He asked me to do my best to teach him English and civilized ways.

Alert and confused, that was my state of mind in those first days I spent on deck with the Yámanas. The first acts of simple curiosity were followed by a devastating fact: Button knew much more than I about anything that came up. He was a better sailor, he had astonishing eyesight and even more astonishing marksmanship with stones; he could be naked in freezing rain or dive into an ice-cold sea; he knew how to hunt and gather shellfish and find cormorant nests on the cliffs; he knew which kind of penguins were not good to eat and where to find fresh water and firewood. He had probably already been with a woman, and, within a year, if he were staying on land, he would be a father. But the young man I was could not at all accept all this. I had taken to heart the job the Captain had delegated to me, and I was always showing him what to do and correcting him.

Like me, in the next two years he was due for another experience: London. And it was there that I would begin to take on meaning in his life, where I would have some advantage over him.

I provided him with clothing and showed him a mirror, which startled him at first but afterwards became an object he consulted constantly. He combined amazing adult skill with childish habits. His eyesight, like that of all his people, was exceptional; a face seen some distance off did not escape him and years later was not forgotten. On deck he would often point to the horizon while the rest of us could not yet see anything, not even a pinpoint, till the Captain brought out his spyglass and was then astonished to discover a crag, a ship, or a whale's tail.

The food was the thing that drew the most admiration from Button and his fellows. That all of us on the ship should have food just like that, not only necessary but accumulated stores, was for them a source of constant wonder. I recall that when they went down to the hold, the ship's stores left them dumbstruck. They went crazy over bread, and they liked the clothes but did not understand the need for them. The thing that literally made Button surrender to the Captain was a pair of gloves he gave him. On deck we enjoyed his amazement for quite some time. That one's hands, independent of the body, should wear their own clothing was something he never could have imagined.

It was common knowledge that the Captain was more and more excited with the idea of taking the Yámanas to London. He had projects which he explained to me in his dry tone; he became involved in plans for their education and, from the beginning, for their religious instruction, which for him was fundamental. He started to speak to Button about the Bible; he showed it to him and turned its pages. He spoke to him about good and evil, sin and virtue, God and the Devil, things that I could see Button interpreted in his own way.

The ship's mission was to survey coasts, islands, bays, and favorable anchorages. Button and I had many opportunities to traverse the country the Yámanas called Wulaia and which he was proud to show me. In a single day its unpredictable climate would change from storm and rain to fair weather with a cold distant sun that made the frozen ground shine and stirred awake unexpected colours in dark forests that descended from the mountaintops to the water's edge. Button loved his country and was proud of its beauty, which I greatly praised. I had marvelled at the snowdrifts, rivers of ice that flowed into bays and fjords which he showed me with ready enthusiasm. Looking for shellfish along the coast one afternoon, I stopped to admire the view and told him in Spanish, with marked emphasis on my words:

"Button's country is beautiful, very beautiful."

Then I repeated it in English and, stretching out an arm, I traced a semicircle that embraced Tierra del Fuego's imposing landscape. Button glanced at me smiling.

"*Hermoso país,*" he repeated in Spanish, then added in English, "Beautiful. Is no Devil in Button's country."

That very afternoon something occurred—it may sound humorous—that shows how naturally Button accepted me even if I felt superior to him. We were walking along a hillside when a sharp stone cut through part of my boot. I had to remove it as well as my sock to see if I was hurt. When he saw my bare foot, Button couldn't hold back a fit of uncontrollable laughter. He could not recover enough to get back his speech. At a loss, I didn't know what was wrong until I realized, not without some chagrin, that he was laughing at my foot. He made himself perfectly understood with signs: my feet were no good, they were the most useless he had ever seen. He would feel my skin and double over laughing. I washed the tiny wound in water, without looking at him. At last I confronted him seriously and said in Spanish:

"Don't make joke, friend."

He made a sign for me to wait, climbed to the first line of trees in the forest and returned with a piece of moss the size of a handkerchief and held it out to me:

"Good. For dry wound." And he repeated, in the same tone I had said it, "Don't make joke, friend."

In those days I was blind. I saw through my own eyes and could hardly gain a glimpse of Button's world. I would also laugh at him along with the other sailors and make obscene jokes about the women's naked bodies. Until one day something happened that initiated a change in me.

I was down in the hold and heard an uproar on deck, Button's strident voice among other voices. I bounded up the steps, fearing that the Captain would reproach me for something wrong done by the Yámanas.

Button was at the stern pacing up and down, gesticulating and pointing to a bulky shape. He seemed insane with fury. To my relief, I noticed that behind his back the members of the crew were laughing. So there was no question of a fight. But Button's feelings were those of a savage, in a primitive state. Within minutes, his anger had impressed them all.

He was accusing one of the men; he would go up to the source of the shouts and then fall back, keeping this up again and again. The seaman had caught a baby seal and some ducklings. This was the bloody heap the Yámana could hardly bear to look at. When he became aware of my presence, he came over and spoke to me, gesturing wildly, a few inches from my face. He made it very clear that such a thing was intolerable, an irreparable wrong had been done, young animals could not be killed, neither the young nor the mothers, and that numerous storms would fall upon us as punishment. Perhaps our ship would sink, and we would all perish at the bottom of the icy strait. I calmed him as much as I could; I led him to the ship's bow, assuring him that the sailor would be punished, but he kept shaking his head.

"Bad, very bad," he repeated disconsolately.

I pretended to worry but smiled to myself at such a fuss. That night a strong wind came up; it whistled in the planking. The whole ship groaned. Awake in my bunk, I remembered the scene of the afternoon. Suddenly, for no reason in particular, I had the sensation that what was happening had to do with something else. Without quite knowing what I would do, I pulled on my boots and went up on deck. I searched for Button and found him squatting near the bow, with his back to the foremast, in darkness barely filtered by the feeble lamp of the prow. He was naked once more, his wet hair flying about his head. Withdrawn, he was staring at a fire on the coast; it danced in the dark, fighting off the wind. A wigwam. Perhaps his family had camped where they could see the ship. What I had sensed was revealed to me there. I went closer and squatted in front of him. I made him look at me.

"Me, Jack," I shouted so he could hear and pointed to my chest, "me never"—and I crossed and uncrossed my hands before my face—"never kill"—I made the mock gesture of clubbing the deck with a stick, joined my hands by the thumbs and made them fly, and measured something of small size with thumb and index finger— "small animals."

He did not utter a word, he made no gesture. He looked me in the eye. I began all over:

"Me, Jack…"

He raised one hand and placed the palm on my chest. He gravely nodded yes.

He had understood, but his mood did not improve. I sat facing him, with my back against the gunwale, determined to show him that I understood. We were in winter, and it was a hard test for me. From time to time the water whipped our faces, and my teeth were chattering. Silent and inscrutable, Button took no notice. At dawn the wind dropped and a strange calm surrounded the ship. With the first glimmer of day, it began to snow. The deck was soon covered with a fine white blanket. I asked Button if he would like to go down and have a mug of coffee. He accepted.

As it took me years to understand, for Button it was not simply a question of mutual sympathy; it didn't end simply with my understanding. On our ship a sacred order superior to us had been transgressed. There was no doubt that there was a punishment nature had only postponed, but which would not be long in coming. Two days later, a wind of hurricane strength with gusts of hail and driving rain shook the ship until it heeled and the Captain had to give the command to weigh anchor. Abrupt changes in the weather are constant in Tierra del Fuego so this was nothing new, but one could see Button's eyes shining with satisfaction. We were receiving the punishment he had predicted, and we deserved it.

There was one seaman on board who, more than any other, liked to amuse himself at Button's expense. He would play low tricks on him and his resulting blunders and errors threw the sailor into wild laughing fits. I was watching the two. We had all seen ample proof of the violence Button and his fellows were capable of. The sailor was foolhardy. Any Yámana was twice as strong as the stoutest man on board; we had been able to confirm this. They would take hold of a man, lift him bodily, and dash him against the rocks. They fought without thinking; it was simply a question of destroying the adversary. Button was a boy, but that violence was latent in him, and this could be seen at a glance. On this day, watching Button come along the deck with the typical rolling gait he had adopted to walk on board, followed by the boisterous laughter of the sailor, I was all attention, prepared to intervene. To my surprise, Button came to me smiling and —I'd swear—mocking. He was shaking his head.

"Too much skylark," he said in English and repeated it before disappearing into the hold, "Too much skylark."

Two years later in England, when Button was already on the farm and speaking English fluently, I learned, a little offended, that the impression I had made on him during those first weeks had been rather unflattering, not to say pathetic.

What's more, he thought I was a little backward and a very slow learner. According to him, he had treated me with "plenty of politeness and patience." He added that it would have amused his people to see how someone so proud of what he knew, who was always trying to teach him things, would turn into a know-nothing as soon as they left him on land for just three days. I was offended, but Button was right.

Let me admit, Mr. MacDowell or MacDowness, that my story cannot be impartial. It could never be. I was Jemmy Button's friend, I developed a fondness for him that grew deep and, with the years, reached its true dimension. At first I felt an undisguised sentiment of superiority to him, but a long time ago I came to understand the parabola of his life and to lament his fate and the fate of his people. The world Button knew, that of his ancestors, was coming to its long end. Like icebergs broken loose from glaciers, his world was beginning to disintegrate and would soon drift toward its own dissolution. My own situation was not very different. We were on the way to a system that had no place for us except the one we had been preassigned. We came from the outer edges of the world, from its ultimate limits, from a barbaric, unimagined place which, in spite of my good English and my blond mop, emanated from me and surrounded me, just as it surrounded Button.


At last we set sail for England. My excitement was equal to what I was, a cabin boy who already felt sure of himself without yet imagining all he still had to learn about the sea. And besides, I was on my way to my father's country, on my way to Mallory's city. The future was opening before me without a cloud on the horizon. I tried to explain to Button where we were headed. He paid little attention to me. As we drew farther away from Wulaia, from its labyrinth of islands and channels, he grew sad and spent hours on deck looking at the last cliffs.

Sailing the high seas disheartened the Yámanas. They were unused to such a long spell on board, and they became morose and silent. We passed briefly through Montevideo, which I reclaimed and abandoned a second time. Button hardly felt like going ashore even once; he didn't seem to respond to the novelty. Only some animals and a few carriages drew him out of his apathy, but even that was momentary. As we sailed north, what affected them mercilessly was what made them sluggish and stripped of vitality: the heat.

Rain is coming down gently to leeward. The coast of Brazil is behind us; ahead, the ocean taking us to an unknown continent. Seated on deck, I let myself relax in the easy rhythmic swaying of the ship. Button looks disconsolately at the last seagulls accompanying us until everything becomes nothing but water. My mind is on what I recall: a cheap brothel very close to the coast, with overhanging eaves and oil lamps flickering in the night wind, and on the mulata I had chosen, yielding, enigmatic, consenting to leave the cots and mats on which drunken sailors were copulating regardless of the kneading bodies around them. Her nude body submissive, her face to the sky, amid the uproar of the tide. The hours on the dark beach where I was a zealous apprentice of everything a man has to learn.

Button had refused to go in and remained sitting on the sand near the fishing boats, looking out to sea. After a few more drinks I had pushed him to the doorless opening of the brothel, accompanied by the mockery of the others. When I returned just before dawn, I saw him going down the beach with a young girl, a mere child whom I had seen inside in the early evening absently waving an outlandishly large leaf, shaped like the ace of spades, with which she was fanning my comrades' heated bodies.

It was my first woman. A mulata. The image of her submission haunts me and I let the blessed rain bathe my face and body. Like a last goodbye, this was the last memory of America that accompanied me and then would disappear, but not forever, with the onslaught of London.

# FOLIO FOUR

The tide set us down like a tray on the river's back. My excitement at the thought of seeing London grew by the hour as we went up the waters of the Thames and approached the city about which the sailors on board had talked tirelessly and which in a way I carried in my blood.

The port was a pandemonium. Montevideo had seemed noisy to me but this was Babel. Ships with unfamiliar flags, enormous warehouses where the shipping clerks shouted at the top of their lungs, tradings, shipments, people from every country and of all races: Negroes, Hindus, Chinese. After all, we were at the heart of the largest sea empire in the world. I couldn't keep track of the scenes going on around me. Button had long ago used up his capacity for astonishment. Or perhaps that capacity was smaller or of a different order than mine. Like his companions he showed a resigned curiosity that was quickly exhausted. He came from a country where the waves were taller than these buildings, where the mornings and the nights last for months, and the whales are as big as sailboats. The chaos of persons, ships, and buildings was irrelevant or made no sense to him. Many of the crew had awaited Button's reaction with curiosity but there was no repetition of the scene that took place when the Captain gave him the pair of gloves that had made him ecstatic. The only thing that made the Yámanas break out of the inhumanity of their cruel displacement was a Negro of giant stature, an Ethiopian brought from Africa, perhaps for a purpose similar to the Captain's. Within a few weeks, dressed in livery and patent leather shoes, his exotic figure would add colour to some London mansion. Now decked out with feathers and necklaces of teeth, he stood as motionless as an idol. His eyes, of watery brilliance, did not even flicker before the inspection of which he was the object. Perhaps the Yámanas were below his line of vision, since they reached far below his shoulder.

Suitably dressed, Button and his companions were taken to an inn near the port, where the Captain rented a room on an upper floor. He ordered me, under threat of punishment, to look after them until his return. Fever had made Boat Memory crumple on deck a few days before and, as soon as he had seen us settled, the Captain took him to the naval hospital. Our progress to the lodgings and our arrival there caused a big stir among people who did not seem to look favourably at the Yámanas. I even thought I heard insults. I had no time to think about the meaning of all the things that were happening. At last I was in the city where Mallory had been born, perhaps even in the very tavern where he had spent a night before shipping out. Thinking about it affected me in a confused and vague manner; it never became a real feeling. His eyes oddly inscrutable, Button lapsed into a silent apathy I couldn't break down. The Yámanas did not like being separated from Boat. The foreboding of his death frightened them. They sat down on the floor against one of the room's walls. I sat beside them, hiding my concern about the growing uproar downstairs. As amusement, some drunken sailors had passed the word around that my companions were cannibals, and there were more and more shouts. A rabble was gathering in the street, and it had turned into more than a bad practical joke. At first the Captain's presence had kept them in line but as soon as he left the ruckus began all over again with alarming violence. I got up quietly and peeked through the shutters. What were we to do if that crowd decided to come upstairs? I could not rely on the innkeeper. The woman had rented us the room unwillingly, hardly won over by the Captain's uniform and generous advance payment.

I took Fuegia's small hand and held it in mine, not only to reassure her but also to see if she was feverish. We had all been vaccinated against smallpox in Montevideo but Boat's case had created persistent alarm. Fortunately, young Fuegia was well. Button's eyes were riveted on mine. What was he trying to tell me? So far every attempt at communication between us had been made by them, and what we could say to each other was thanks to their incredible mimetic skill; I knew only one or two words of their language. I pointed to the locked door.

"The Captain will return soon and we shall leave this house," I said partly in English, partly in sign language.

However, that was not all. Sitting in a corner on the floor, pressed together as in the winter of their remote country, there was no wigwam made of poles or branches over their heads, there was no familiar wind dashing the sea against the rocks, there were no dogs to give men their friendly body heat, nor did tongues of immemorial fire rise around them. Here there was only confusion and fear and men shouting below, gone mad. Instinct told them that they had to stay close together without moving, because they were in strange territory and around them there raged an unknown and savage enemy. Only Fuegia's childish voice dared cut through the cold semi-darkness.

"Like sea lion hunters," she said.

And in her round face her serious eyes brought into that room images of brutality and murder.

I too was restless. I wanted to imagine that I could carry out the Captain's orders, but the truth is that the one place where I felt safe was in the room with the Yámanas.

Some hours later, there were only a few braggarts left; for them the Yámanas had been the day's scandal and they were unwilling to leave us in peace. I decided to go down for something to eat. There was a surprise in store for me. One of those who wanted to teach us a lesson us was waiting at the foot of the stairs.

He was a nobody in a frayed greasy black outfit. A few filthy strands of hair and bushy sideburns stuck out under his hat. He started shouting as soon as he saw me.

"Bring down the cannibals! Throw the guttersnipes out!"
He came towards me and spat on the floor.

The innkeeper pretended not to notice. The nobody kept up his insults.

"To jail with the cannibals! Let them rot in the hole! They must be carted off to jail right now!"

This time I didn't let him come closer. I am not now nor was I at eighteen a small man, Mr. MacDowell or MacDowness, and the Englishman was built like a dried herring. I shoved him by the shoulders: I hardly touched him and he flew against the tables and then lay sprawled on the floor. Two others in back threatened to get up. I thought of the Captain and my future. We might end up in jail without having been in London twenty-four hours.

"Sorry, mister," I mumbled. I picked him up bodily by his lapels and pretended to dust off his clothes. "We had all better take it easy, lest the cannibals become restless. The Captain will be back tomorrow," I lied to the fat toothless hag. "We shall be leaving soon."

For some reason, the bullies disappeared. The innkeeper reluctantly handed me some plates with a stew I didn't even want to look at. I didn't like what I was seeing of London, and I liked its inhabitants even less. In Lobos I had never seen such filthy people.

I went back to the room. No one ate. It was cold at daybreak and I wrapped myself in a blanket that the Yámanas, with eyes wide open in the dark, had refused to accept. Despite the apparent peace that now reigned below, York, Fuegia, and Button did not change position, not even to look inside the bureau or the wardrobe, which in other circumstances would have aroused their admiration. On the following days, I took heart and went out, venturing a little farther each day. At nightfall I would return to the inn and the sensation of elation caused by my first wanderings in the city would dissipate and be replaced by guilt. Upstairs, left to themselves, silent strangers, the Yámanas awaited my return as the only link that joined them to a world that wanted nothing to do with them.

With the Yámanas in London, Mr. MacDowell or Mac-Downess, an unavoidable question came up. Why had they been brought there? At the time, I hardly could have thought it over with absolute clarity, but the question hung palpably in the air and could not be ignored. The Captain had decided to bring them and his absence ruled out any definite answer. They had been brought for nothing. They had been forced to cross the ocean on a whim or to carry out an experiment, and I could not get to the bottom of it.

Time would lead me to understand that the purpose of Button's presence in London was being decided very far from there, far above the port's filthy streets and persons like us: in the lofty and inaccessible circles of power, where England worked out its designs throughout the world. The Yámanas occupied a very precise space in a complicated jigsaw puzzle, one of whose pieces was the coveted Tierra del Fuego with its channels opening into the Pacific.


The pampa wind blows with more and more force. The horizon, which was bright a few minutes ago has now turned violet, and an immense slate-colored cigar, stretched out on the line of the horizon, is rolling quickly toward us. In the clarity still around us the birds appear to have gone insane and are flying from place to place, crisscrossing, seeking refuge from impending danger. In the increasing darkness the distant rumble of thunder begins. A restless Ajax hides under the table. Graciana bolts the rattling doors, which have begun to shake. I've gone over to the window to watch the spectacle. The thistle patch waves furiously, the treetops are shaken mercilessly; all at once the water comes down with brute force, while night moves in and the plain rumbles as if a stampede of runaway horses were coming up the immense corridor of the plateau from far south. What frightened me as a boy thrills me as a man. A storm on the pampa, Mr. MacDowell or MacDowness, is something you couldn't possibly imagine in the narrow space of your small office: it feels as if the entire house will be pulled up by its foundations —and suddenly it's all over. The thunderclaps and the lightning stop, the rain suddenly ceases, and a supernatural brightness opens in the sky and bathes the plain with such vivid and delicate colors that only a man like your Turner, extraordinarily sensitive to light, could describe. Life starts anew and as in the first moment of the Creation, harmony reigns in the four directions of the pampa.

Graciana has opened the doors again. I stop writing because, with the storm past, outside the afternoon beckons us to come out.

On the fourth day, the Captain came back for the Yámanas. He sent Fuegia and York to a farm in the country, where they would receive an English education and the rudiments of certain skills. Button would remain with me in London for a few weeks, then would also be taken to the farm-school. This separation caused no problems; York's protective instinct toward Fuegia had become evident.

"He is waiting for her to grow up," Button explained to me.

The Captain bought Jemmy new clothes, and got him a haircut and boots. He even presented him with a hat. With much effort, Button had gotten past his first week in England and was gradually appearing interested and curious once more. The winter cold contributed to this attitude. The three of us would go out in the Captain's carriage. At first Button wanted to ride sitting next to the coachman who every now and then would let him have the reins. He had recovered his astonishing mimetic skill and nothing physical was hard for him to learn. It was something else with certain actions, in which he was utterly lost. Button's disconcerting questions demonstrated how confusing were relationships that were normal to the whites. Their inconsistency confused him. To talk for the sake of talking or to insist on things that later did not prove to be true disconcerted him. That there should be veiled intentions behind certain actions disappointed and confused him. But, as the Captain liked to repeat, he was very intelligent and he adjusted.

One afternoon the Captain spent quite some time showing him paper money and coins.

"Money," he would say, separating coins of different value. "Money for trade, to buy things."

I had taken a hat which I exchanged with the Captain for a coin. The Captain gave me back small coins. This mimicry was followed seriously, with concentration, by Button who, nevertheless, for a moment looked into my eyes questioningly and then looked at the Captain again with interest. Button nodded assent, asked for the money, and repeated the operation with me. He understood the act of exchanging long before we had ended our pompous demonstration. The abstract value of money was something else. The idea of possessing it for its own sake pertained to a world of immaterial values, of mysterious influence that Button was never able to assimilate. Or perhaps he did, in a way, as what follows will illustrate.

We were strolling along crowded streets near the port. The Captain had given him several coins that he put in his pocket. They were given as a test to see if it would occur to him to buy something. Button took them out of his pocket and was busy polishing them on his jacket, throwing them up in the air and catching them again as he had seen me doing. One got away from him and went rolling over the cobblestones. All at once a group of ragged urchins rushed out of the entryways and fell upon the coin. This amazed and delighted him. Screaming, the thin dirty faces turned toward us hoping for more. Truly delighted, he threw a second coin into the air, and this produced a huge commotion. Button was laughing next to those children who now surrounded him and pulled at his clothes. When I saw that he meant to throw all he had into the street, I grabbed his arm, but he broke loose without violence.

"Very amusing, Jack," he said laughing. "Very amusing!"

That's how Button lost the only money he ever had but gained an extraordinary experience: he was able to conceive the abstract idea of the power that money confers. From then on he only asked for coins in order to throw them into the street. For a Yámana the idea of buying any object or food was inconceivable; in Cape Horn each individual obtains what he needs, and the rest belongs to everyone, but this, among many other things, no one had ever bothered to find out.

Since the Captain deemed the handling of money essential, when he left for his home he ordered me to keep insisting. Happy to be able to walk about by ourselves in a city or at least in neighborhoods where we now felt at home, we used to go out into the streets among the people to do more or less what we had to. With this idea I walked into a shop to buy a pipe and some tobacco, improving on the demonstration by insistent and elaborate bargaining that amused me. Button followed the counting of the coins and the argument over the price with the attention of a diligent student. But later he said to me:

"Money, Jack; money to throw."

He had held up a coin in front of my face and indicated with signs, exactly as we had done with him, that I was to throw it into the street among the little fellows.

Soon we were popular; we were a pair of odd types, permanently followed by a bunch of screaming children. Button liked it; in his country special consideration was shown to children—one's own as well as others'—whom everyone without exception looked after with a zeal that could reach the point of sacrifice.

To Button, London's filthy ragamuffins were the least threatening and most intelligible thing about England.

Going up and down the streets of London, two parallel pictures of poverty that seemed hopeless took shape in my mind: that of my country's endless plains—where we are reduced to a state of permanent poverty, partly because of our rejection of manual labour, and partly because, except for war, no one knew what to hire us for—and that of London. The crowding together of a multitude in houses which looked like basements, black as caves, oozing dampness, was no improvement over the desert I had left. In these houses women with sunken breasts gave birth to skinny children they cast out into the streets and who no sooner learned to walk than they had to carry the next one born. London revealed a poverty I hadn't known. In my country perhaps we were more barbaric and poorer, but, I dared think, happier. In London I recalled the storms that cleaned out the pampa and carried poverty and plagues far away. In these neighborhoods disease and misery had settled into the very cobblestones.

It was an extraordinary experience, Mr. MacDowell or MacDowness: unpromising and devastating at the same time. Since I had grown up in the desert, that aimless multitude which earned its daily bread any way it could, with dirty schemes and clandestine undertakings, attracted me like a whirlpool to its centre.

Many years later I would be able to associate those painful scenes—that returned like fist blows to my face—with these verses of Shelley's that I did not know then: *Hell is a city much like London–/a populous and a smoky city;/ there are all sorts of people undone,/...Small justice shown, and still less pity...*, lines which, by chance, memory joins tonight, thousands of miles away in the pampa, to others that come—I don't recall their source—of their own free will: *I wander through each chartered street,/Near where the chartered Thames does flow,/And mark in every face I meet/ Marks of weakness, marks of woe.* For whom, I asked myself innocently, were the riches and dominions that the English conquered and held on to at any price in the most remote corners of the planet? The neighborhoods which succeeded one another interminably down the narrow cobbled streets were not inhabited by the beneficiaries of those enterprises.

Mallory had trotted down those streets, and any of those dark entryways might have been his.

None of our long walks could intimidate Button. We roamed the streets of the never-ending city from morning till night. Two bodies among thousands of nameless unfamiliar bodies, excitable, happy, glum, miserable human beings whose faces we were seeing for the first and last times and were dragging us from one street to the next street down a labyrinth which sometimes ended abruptly in dead-end walls blackened by time and smoke. Our London seemed to drift toward the waterfront where the city was restive. Night would fall on the Thames and we would hover about the bridges. The trembling water near the docks mirrored a city resplendent with thousands of gaslights. Of course, we lost our way and slept anywhere: in parks, entryways, markets, near the riverside. As we left behind our natural territory—the waterfront or the outlying industrial districts—those places were taken over by beggars, ragpickers, decrepit old women, the blind, and the crippled, who lingered at church doors. Their begging took place at night. With daylight, those beings retreated to their burrows and vanished from the places where the city opened into avenues and parks, and where their presence would be an ugly blot on those residential walls behind which the Captain moved, where his relatives and friends were, and where he had influence.

Being one and the same, this was a different city. Its magnificent architecture left me dumbfounded. Dragging Button behind me, time and again I trudged the streets around those palaces and gardens as if they were another country.

Before those dazzling marble walls surrounded by tree-lined avenues, before those carriages whose horses no doubt led more sheltered lives than the people on those dirty corners from which we came, Button and I dissolved, we became nothing. We came from a place that was not only unimaginable here—the roar of the wind, the endless prairie, the bonfires at night, the whale hunt—but even if they had known it, nobody cared. What continued undisturbed was the aristocratic indifference, more solid and imposing than the walls, the huge arches and portals. We were nobodies, pure and simple.

Our existence began to materialize in another part of the city, in the Colonial Offices, in the Stock Exchange, in the Admiralty. There, through a strange alchemy of civilization, Button and I assumed our bodies, we became real, we belonged somewhere on the globe that was perfectly situated and transformed us into skins, oil, numbers.

I can't say that I wasn't learning. The monumentality of London annulled yet educated me, raised me toward itself. I was sensitive to its undeniable beauty. There was much to be learned from its landscaped gardens and the gaslights, not from these in themselves but from the thinking that had made them possible. In London, like in conches, Mr. MacDowell or MacDowness, time could be seen. Time was stamped in stone, in iron and in marble. And it was not only the buildings; people also occupied a place in the stratified flow of decades and centuries. Their clothes, carriages and houses gave an estimate of who they were, their rank and their past, what they expected from life and what life had conceded them beforehand.

Time did not exist where we came from, no one knew how it had passed, because life always seemed to return to the earth without leaving a trace. Facts had to be tied down to the plain to keep them from flying off. History had yet to begin, while there in London the years, centuries, past ages receded at a dizzy pace simply through the act of looking.

I did not understand very much, but I understood enough to realize that my spirit had remained trapped between an unfathomable and deserted nature and the swarming multitude of a city to which there seemed to be no end.

England was teaching me, and I, like a huge fish, was swallowing everything.

Button, however, could neither see nor understand it. It wasn't even possible for him to even begin to understand what all this signified. He had nowhere to take what he saw. Whom could Button tell about his experience with gardens, inns, or money and, above all, to whom could he explain the meaning of what he was seeing: a city that glowed at night with a thousand lights that were multiplied in the river? If Button had wanted to describe it, he would have expressed it with sound and fury, and his story would be an endless description of circumstances and objects presented by someone able to see what was going on but unable to understand why.

Years later I confirmed that what the little doctor had called "Button's regression to a savage state" described perfectly Button's response to his contact with civilization. The best possible, the only response.

I have spent a sleepless night, Mr. MacDowell or Mac-Downess. Really quite restless. My memory of London, of the many occasions I was in it, which I condense in a description of my first visit there since other small details would only lead to an account with little interest, inclines me to consider other things.

Last night, by the light of the kerosene lamp, rummaging through the leather trunk I've always had with me during the last thirty years, filled with objects of all kinds—mementos from countries I'll never visit again, the harpoon made of bone which Jemmy Button gave me, the scrapbook with notes about that long-ago passage—, I found what I was looking for: some old newspapers that force of habit has made me continue to get from Buenos Aires. I'm talking about the *Times*. Its pages, and specifically certain paragraphs from a copy of one from 1859, may illustrate how the end of the earth from which we came was seen from "the centre of the maritime Empire." The article mentions the Patagonian Mission. The missionary mystique was, definitely and as I believe I've already said, the cause that set loose the chain of events for which Jemmy Button was tried in the Islands.

I translate part of what the *Times* says: "As we can see, the missionary spirit is often associated with the spirit of romantic adventure. A distant country on the other side of the Equator, wrapped in the mystery of another hemisphere, savage tribes, still unknown, whose minds are a *tierra incognita* for us, arouse an interest and a curiosity that relieve the monotony of the everyday world.

"We do not censure that mixture of religion and romantic spirit, which is perfectly natural. But it is obvious that such a spirit of religious adventure is accompanied by risks that the Patagonian Missionary Society did not foresee. No one can question the enthusiasm and zeal of this association and the truly generous character that pointed out the mysterious coasts of Tierra del Fuego as the field for a missionary undertaking.

"All that could be desired for a religious adventure was there: aboriginal savagery was enthroned there beneath clouds the light had never penetrated, a land of spirits or phantoms. The country of Herodotus's barbarians and the other where it rained feathers could hardly outdo Tierra del Fuego with its unknown enchantment.

"And yet this religious expedition, planned under a halo of romantic and spiritual adventure, was from the beginning destined for trouble. As soon as they arrived at one of the Falkland Islands, they clashed with the then Governor, Mr. Rennie.

"Captain Parker Snow (hired to pilot the Mission's ship, the schooner *Allen Gardiner)*, in spite of his objections to the Mission's methods, made the crossing to Tierra del Fuego in search of future converts and was successful in finding Jemmy Button, a native whose familiar name identifies him as an old acquaintance. Later on, the Mission's minister plenipotentiary, the Reverend Despard, confronted Captain Parker Snow and relieved him of his charge. From the manner in which Captain Snow later referred to his employers, one might suppose that they were heathen Turks or monsters instead of devout and zealous missionaries.

"These unfortunate results would have been avoided if those good people had not failed to make the slightest investigation or had prepared themselves for the difficulties in store. All they imagined were bucolic scenes of savage life: Patagonian chiefs subject to missionary dominion and the awakening of barbarian minds.

"It is now known that the Patagonian Mission ended badly, and not only were the pagans not converted but the outcome was a quarrel within a group of excellent Christians."


As can be inferred from the opinion of the *Times*, Mr. MacDowell or MacDowness, no specific Button was really seen by those in the city we were learning to know.

The article has reminded me of something. The word "romantic" was fashionable at the time, was used for everything. Here it is well employed; it gives the undertaking the superficial, not to say irresponsible, aspect it had. You, or whosoever lays eyes someday on these disordered pages, can draw your own conclusions.

Allow me to go on telling my own story.

In London I was blindly looking for the name of a neighborhood or a street that would rescue from my memory something said on some occasion by Mallory. I looked in at doorways and asked in taverns. Or perhaps this is not quite true, perhaps I did not want to find anything, and the search only gave me an excuse to wander all day long and go into places which otherwise I would never have been able to enter. The thing I never learned was what Button found in those streets.

One afternoon we crossed the threshold of an elegant shop where they sold clothes of the kind worn by gentlemen like the Captain. Button stopped short before several pairs of gloves on display.

"Did you know a man anywhere around here with the last name of Mallory? He lived on this street." I made this up for the clerk, an elegant type who was staring horrified at Button. "You may remember him; he's an admiral in the Navy."

They threw us out immediately but not before I had pocketed a pair of gloves on the sly. Button deserved them. From the beginning, even during the passage, I had explained to him what I was looking for, and he had wholeheartedly offered to go with me. Even when we spent all day wandering about, his willingness did not diminish. Things like the one I've just told you occurred not only once but many times. Actually, shortly after leaving the neighborhood near the waterfront, the worthy plan of finding my father's house was forgotten in the constant discovery of new things.

Hours later, stopping at the stand of a woman selling oysters or looking at some kids on barges along the river, suddenly Button would take my arm:

"Finding father very important."

I nodded and we would move on to other places we were not acquainted with.

One evening in a tavern I had gone to alone—Button did not like taverns—something occurred that, without doubt, I was waiting to happen as if by magic.

Amidst the smoke and the noisy swearing typical of men enjoying themselves, and in whose company I proudly wished to belong, I was at a table drinking when a man who was down at the heel but imposing and rather drunk, to whom I had confided that my father was English, asked me his last name.

"His name was Mallory," I said. "William Mallory."

The man opened his eyes.

"Might it be one who ended up joining the Navy?" he asked, leaning across the table.

"The same one," I answered without hesitating. Thousands had gone to sea and thousands were still doing it, but something like this had not even entered my mind.

The man let out a horse laugh.

"Mallory! William Scott Mallory! Did I know him?" He exclaimed. "I knew that scoundrel when he and I ran around London! We got into a lot of fights together. Earning a living in these streets was hard, son. William Scott Mallory, why of course. What became of that son of a bitch, boy?"

"He died. Over two years ago."

The man shook his head sadly:

"Our turn comes sooner or later, yes sir. In bed or in the water, but it comes." He quickly recovered his good mood. "We used to make the rounds of the taverns trying to find something, anything that came our way…"

I hung on to his words. The man was growing merrier in the warmth of an invisible fireplace. He swallowed half a pitcher and brought the palm of his hand down hard on the table.

"How he used to bore the shit out of me with some chap called Milton…! He was in the habit of stealing useless things, like books. By St. Elmo, what a strange habit…!"

I could merely stutter that yes, it had to be my father, when the man, having quickly caught on to my impatience, suddenly seemed to remember everything and began a story in which there was a certain Charles Mallory, apparently my father's uncle.

"He lived not far from here, with his uncle Charles, an old man completely out of his mind, boy. Your father took me to his diggings." My new friend flashed the big smile of a good-hearted pirate, his jaw jutted out, and he tapped his throat softly. "Talking makes my pipes dry up…" he said, pointing to the empty wine pitchers.

I called the tavern keeper. No one was interested in his story, except me, and we soon had the table to ourselves. My companion put away half of another pitcher at one swig.

"Sure, the old man was balmy but a very good man. Poor Scotty would have starved to death without him." He leaned his elbows on the table, all set to feed me a story or invent one, and I was ready to believe it all and pay for all the drinks needed to let me hear it out. He half-closed his eyes:

"Mallory had been left an orphan almost at birth, and this uncle Charles Mallory had raised him. The old man seemed to be book-crazy; I never saw anything like it in all my life. They were piled up in every corner. I always thought a good fire could start up there. They would have been roasted alive, boy, if a flying spark had hit there; they would have burned, yessir, like oakum."

"But my father, what did he do?"

"What could he do? He had to obey the old man. Mallory, your father, boy, used to run around the streets like me, looking for something, anything to keep us alive. And it would have been natural, but the thing is he would get orders to procure some book. So he stole them. Old man Charles was almost blind and he gave him house and food on condition that he read to him out loud. So your father, from the time he was small, was like at Oxford, reading helter-skelter, in the daytime or with a candle. The old man always wanted more stories, more books. Scotty must have been your age when old Charlie died on us. Then he went to sea and I lost sight of 'im…"

I don't know how to describe the excitement this meeting produced in me. Mallory's supposed friend had put together a story that explained many things to me.

"My father and I read many books together. Look," I started to rummage in my bag and pulled out what I had gotten that same afternoon. I held up the two little books, *"The Swan of Avon!"* I added with stupid pedantry I'm now ashamed of. "He liked Ben Jonson but I…"

"That's it, that's it." The man interrupted me drawing back in his chair. "That was Mallory, boy." He looked at me annoyed, blinking an eye and twisting his mouth, as if instead of showing him books I was holding up a dead rat. He studied me. His eyes told me what he was thinking: what was I, a ridiculous and greenhorn showoff, doing with all my big talk about books in an honest tavern for simple people? He hooked his thumbs into the cord that was holding up his pants. He had what is called a prominent abdomen. He came a little closer and peered into the pitcher.

"Tavern keeper!" I shouted.

"Yes, I can almost see him," he spoke again in a jovial mood. "Good old William Scott Mallory! He would go from table to table reciting and talking about Ben Jonson. It has stayed up here," he pointed to his brow. "How he bored the damnation out of us with that Ben Jonson and a certain John Milton! We were great friends, me boy. And I'll tell you something: yes, you look like him…"

I felt a knot in my throat and I took a good drink. My companion did the same. His face was purple; he pumped air into his lungs.

"Once, I remember now, once, in one of those rich neighborhoods, he stayed locked up all night in a public library. He was able to get away with a few books. Old Charlie was so happy that he nearly kicked the bucket... That's what he was like, old Charles Mallory, your grandfather, boy."

"My granduncle," I said as clearly as I could.

"The very same."

A little dizzy but happy and satisfied, and encouraged by my comrade's good mood, I was ready to order another pitcher. Destiny, however, did not intend that night to end in a peaceful way. As if drawn by our frequent mentioning of him, Mallory's spirit made itself felt, and the evening turned into a battle royal. In effect, at the least expected moment, in the midst of the thick smoke and the heavy atmosphere of the place, someone jumped up from I don't know where and for some reason started to insult my friend who, at this point, was too drunk to stand.

The stranger had seized him by the neck and at the top of his voice was calling him thief, among other ugly slurs that I, not any more sober, took as aimed at me. A circle soon formed in the midst of the commotion of overturned tables and pitchers flying through the air. I don't know how I found myself in the centre apparently determined to give my life for Mallory's friend who showed signs of being offended but was in a hurry to reach the street. In the meantime the man wronged by a theft I knew nothing about had pulled out a knife. This move produced a momentary silence among those present and had on me a considerable effect that cleared my head somewhat. I had just enough time to pull a jacket from the back of a chair and wrap it around my left arm like a poncho. Before I had time to think, the wild man—who had aimed several stabs at me, parried by me God knows how— had cut my arm above the elbow. A minute later the fight was over: I took flying aim at him with a bottle, made a feint at his stomach and smashed the bottle on his head. There was tremendous cheering all around. They poured gin on my wound and bandaged it more or less adequately among hurrahs and whiskies.

Mallory's friend hugged me, visibly moved:

"Just like your father, boy! Where did you learn to defend yourself like that? Just like your father!" he kept saying.

Hours later I left the tavern drunk as a lord, singing truculent lyrics at the top of my lungs, hanging on to my new friend so as not to fall.

I now had a family tree.


Button was taken to the country school; I was left to myself and spent little time at my lodgings. At night I went out compulsively. A deafening and disorderly tumult reigned there, it was the hour when the taverns were brimming over with sailors, merchants, thieves, and prostitutes. The milling crowds and the confusion excited me, stirred in me a happy mood impossible to explain. We were all engulfed in the same ill-smelling human warmth which made us think the night would last forever. Instead of the silent, dull horizon of the pampa, an ant heap of bodies and faces formed one multiple entity caught in the same frenzy. Only much later, the raw light of morning would restore those outlying places and streets to their real nature. In the meantime there, a few steps away from the calm waters of the Thames, for a few hours one could put off the bitter knowledge that life was a trap from which few managed to escape. This desperate spree created a vibrant aura, a halo of misery, like St. Elmo's fires above the masts during a storm. It was the meeting place of those who manage to survive as best they can, those who have nothing to lose, a breed whose very sordidness and ugliness fascinated me, because I was beginning to know, Mr. MacDowell or MacDowness, in a way I can't explain, that it was nothing but the human condition. This and not the Captain, the boatswain, the gentlemen with clean-shaven rosy complexions and neat decent suits, not the well-educated teachers and proud ladies with whom the men visiting the Captain's home spoke and drank tea on the porches. The human condition was not seen there, owing perhaps to the inordinate display of clothes or elegance or refinement. Walking London's streets, lost in the multitude, in that anonymous stream of bodies, no doubt with much wine under my belt, I would say to myself: But wasn't the Captain perhaps also a man, and furthermore a decent educated man? Hadn't he invented an instrument to detect storms at sea? Didn't he read the Bible to his crew for solace? Wasn't that something human or for the benefit of humans, and, in consequence, didn't that place the Captain in the category I felt was "the human condition"? Somehow, for the boy I was at the time, this did not form an answer. Arbitrarily, I felt that the Captain was too wealthy and influential, too educated. In the streets, the taverns, the street stalls—as aboard ship—one could see brutal and degenerate faces, it's true, but these were places where one could also see faces capable of understanding everything, unusual signs of solidarity and brotherly feeling that shone out like polished stones in a mud hole. I was convinced that if any of those grand ladies and gentlemen I had glimpsed in the other London of luxurious and spacious abodes, if any of them had been cast out into these streets without their possessions—with nothing but what they had on—, like any one of us, they would soon have come to that extreme condition with the vital need to survive. And yet if these same drunkards, these prostitutes, and these beggars, in whom I sensed the true human condition, had found themselves face to face with the nude Buttons of Cape Horn, they would no doubt have stoned them, calling them cannibals, not caring that there was a small girl among them. They would have driven them into the sea, thinking they had the right to do it simply because they felt superior.

The Empire, Mr. MacDowell or MacDowness, can't help but reproduce its own. Power engenders the evil-minded who ill-treat the needy in all parts of the world. This is something that can never be said of the Yámanas or Button and his sons, considered the instigators of the massacre for which they were tried in the Islands, and which is why you sent me your letter. They are the neediest in Tierra del Fuego. They live and survive and their struggle is simple and natural, and I would even say heroic in those desolate places. The life of their community comes before the individual and consequently there is no room for deceit or exploitation or rejection. In my country the devil does not exist, Button once said to me.

Tonight the wine has gone to my head. Not the wine of the taverns of my youth but the one on this lonely table in the middle of the lonely pampa. Writing and wine do not go hand in hand; alcohol exaggerates, distorts images. It's wise to stop writing now and let eloquence be appeased by sleep.

Graciana is asleep on her cot. By candlelight the wildness of her tousled hair stands out against the childish peacefulness of her face…

All because of my drowsiness or her girlish body.

One morning the Captain turned up unexpectedly at the inn near the waterfront. For several days, since the extravagant drinking spree and the fight, I had not gone out. Apparently worried about my health, some companions who also lived there or in places close by, had advised me to slow down, the Captain was against excesses and if there were another voyage I might miss it. This had a magic effect in calming me. I spent my time reading what I had acquired.

My room itself was dreary but the general disorder converted it into a lair that matched my appalling aspect. In the doorway, that morning, the Captain screwed up his nose; he seemed better turned out and more elegant than ever. I jumped to my feet.

"You have been among savages so long that you've become one. I'll be downstairs in an hour, and I want you to go with me."

An hour later, clean, decently dressed, and with even a

hasty haircut that the fat innkeeper had agreed to give me, I sat down beside the Captain, who ordered his coachman:

"To the Admiralty."

We crossed to the other city and, carriage and all, we went into an impressive building. A liveried lackey opened the door for us. The Captain appeared tense. Difficult negotiations made him come and go from his residence in the suburbs to this building, the centre of all his problems. His family had always been part of the most influential circle of English politics, but the Captain preferred the sea. He did not move at ease among palace intrigues and power. In my opinion, the men on the other side, who handled politics, found him too proud and inflexible.

From what he told me during our short ride, he was trying to obtain permission to sail to Tierra del Fuego once more. He had decided to take the Yámanas back but he didn't tell me why. He explained that he had been expecting official support for months, but if he didn't get it, he would finance the passage himself.

I stayed in a hallway looking at the marble floors and balustrades, the staircase a full ship's crew could have walked up shoulder to shoulder. I also saw several subalterns' offices—probably like the one you occupy, Mr. MacDowell or MacDowness—which an usher, flattered by my admiration, agreed to show me. After awhile, the Captain came out. A group of men, some in uniform and others in civilian clothes, surrounded him. Speaking in low tones, the group advanced like a procession, with the Captain in the centre. He appeared to be considerably upset, not to say angry, hardly able to keep up his good manners. I couldn't stop regarding them with a curious eye: they were the powerful of this earth. They didn't impress me very much. Their slow walk down the hallways, between ushers who bowed to them, was accompanied by whispers. I realized it was intended to please the Captain, to keep him from leaving in anger; it must have been an extraordinary concession, one accorded only to the most illustrious visitors. This gesture did not dispel the bad humor of the Captain who, once he was in the carriage, locked himself in a glacial silence.

A minute before leaving me at the inn, he informed me, almost as if he were talking to himself, that they had refused his request. At the moment, the Far East claimed all their attention, and the Admiralty had neither time nor money to spare for Tierra del Fuego. And much less, for three savages.

London was a coffer filled with surprising gifts. I had been with women from the taverns, but one night I met Isabella.

Quite drunk, I had approached a young woman with whom I went on drinking until we went upstairs, I don't know how, to a room and a bed where, as in a pleasant dream, I saw myself repeating a frequent scene in the life of Mallory. That's how fast and unforeseen it was. I found myself sitting on a bed, with my head almost touching the ceiling—which sloped down low—and watching a woman undress, who by the light of a candle offered me an amazingly beautiful and slender body. She came naked to where I was, came slowly, letting herself be stared at while she in turn stared at me with laughing eyes. Her skin, so fine and warm, left me speechless, reduced to my sense of touch. Throwing herself upon me in the bed, she whispered under her breath that I could do with her anything I desired, I could beat her if I so wished. If I liked, I could whip her and do other things I can't remember, but they went to my head faster than the wine had. She was eager to please and at the same time elusive, she was a whore who made love for money, but she was the most precious gift the city lavished on me, the city I swore that night never to leave.

I spent four days with Isabella. I'm not lying, Mr. MacDowell or MacDowness, when I tell you that it is one of the few beautiful memories in my life. She was generous and I was generous. A delivery boy went up and down the stairs with drinks and food, for I believe we were naked all this time. At daybreak, lying face down on the bed, with our arms and faces resting on that garret's windowsill, we would remain looking out into the deserted streets and the roofs of that miserable neighborhood, in its own way mysterious by the light of the moon. In the quiet of those dawns, we told each other our lives. For my part, I exaggerated some facts and added details that made me look good; the sincere thing was happiness, life reduced to this room and Isabella, and the rest could fall apart without my batting an eye. As for her, her story needed no embroidery. She was sixteen and had been raised by her grandmother, whose name she had inherited, but whom they called the Venetian.

Sitting like a Moor on the unmade bed, her dark hair over porcelain-like breasts, she told as if it were a fairy tale what had been told to her from the time she first had the use of reason. The Venetian was a beautiful woman who said she was a duke's daughter. She said her home had been a palace from which she could see the boats rocking in the Grand Canal, that she had had forty servants and fancy clothes, that she had been betrothed to a prince and that she traveled to church by water. The only relic of that life was a cameo on which, looked at carefully—Isabella made me bring my face close to the candle's light while she held up the diminutive pendant—one could see a crown and under it an illegible inscription. Kidnapped at the age of fourteen by pirates from the Adriatic, after being sold around to various ships, the other Isabella had become the favorite mistress of Cook, the famous navigator, and had made long voyages with him. At nineteen—by then well known in ports as the Venetian—the old Isabella had been left in Plymouth and from then on she had managed to survive, one way or another, until she arrived in London.

Everyone said she was crazy, but she was well-liked for her generous heart and admired for her disposition. She had given birth to a daughter by an unknown father and, when it became necessary, she had also brought up her granddaughter whom she named Isabella, since her mother had died in childbirth. The Venetian was in the habit of making the rounds of the waterside taverns, taking her granddaughter along. Her biggest vice—men were something else, business or the means to make a living—was cigars, which she had learned to smoke on her passages with Cook to certain islands with crushing heat and skies so blue and clear that young Isabella couldn't possibly imagine them. Nor could she imagine what a tree called a palm was like.

On those savage islands, the Venetian would tell her granddaughter, she used to walk half naked along the shore with Cook, smoking cigars and blowing puffs of smoke into the burning air. In a tent improvised on the beach, by the light of torches, the ship's cook would prepare a fish soup recommended for its aphrodisiac qualities.

Isabella wanted to know if there were cigars and palm trees where I came from.

To let her go on talking and not leave me, I invented things I had never seen. I combined gauchos on horseback with the three or four Brazilians I had come across in my life, I made them all smoke huge cigars, and I told her I would like to meet the Venetian. Isabella laughed. I had already met her. I had been so drunk that I didn't remember it. The Venetian was very fussy about picking out men for young Isabella. For some reason, I had seemed to her a suitable customer, after which, making sure I had money to pay, she had disappeared.

I wanted to know what had become of Cook.

The paradise with Cook ended one morning with atrocities, about which the Venetian remembered three things: the lifeless body of the mariner surrounded by tattooed savages, her escape to the ship with those who had survived, and a strange name that Isabella pronounced with reverence and fear: Kalakakoa.

I slept through the fifth day. When I woke up, Isabella had vanished with the little I had left.

This seemed right to me. That is how in England I ended up spending the silver coins which had been Mallory's military wages for an invasion that had failed. They had been my inheritance, and I had just gone through them in a way that perhaps would not have displeased him.

For several days now this story has been dragging me along and I've left the papers only to eat something at the insistence of Graciana, who asks me whether I am sick, and to sleep at intervals, lying carelessly in my cot.

Writing has strange effects, Mr. MacDowell or Mac-Downess. No doubt driven by what I told you a few days ago, the day before yesterday I saddled a horse and galloped to the store. I wanted to see the old man. He was there as usual, in his corner between the back wall and the counter. Toes the color of the earthen floor, mummified, protruded from his horsehide boots. His small watery eyes can hardly see any longer, and I didn't know if he remembered me.

In answer to my question, he remained silent; when I thought he had already forgotten me, a tiny rasping voice came from his throat.

"The major...sure enough. Many years back, around the year 10 or 12, he built his house. He brought along a woman," he stared into the air. "The gringo was something to behold in the countryside...he went into the pampas to fight dressed like the English..."

He said nothing more. Then he added:

"That was something."

I ordered another round for both of us and lit my pipe. Inside they were preparing the stew. I stayed a long while leaning on my elbows next to the old man, watching through the door as night came down, watching them light the oil lamps, forgetting everything, when I once again heard the small cracked voice.

"Did you know' im?"

I paused a moment before that face grooved with wrinkles, where the clouded beady eyes were somehow watching me.

"No," I finally said. "Matter of fact, I didn't."

When I returned, it was pitch black. I went back without stopping. Far off, the moon lit up the surface of the lagoon.


Weeks passed and I grew discouraged. What the Captain had said made uncertain my future as well as that of the Yámanas. I missed them, especially Button. As the months went by, London seemed monstrous, and everything I had found exciting at first made me sad now. Except for my shipmates, I had no one there. I had found nothing, not a sign of the personal glory that sometimes on deck, watching the clouds run over the moon, the boy I then was had imagined that the world held in store for him. What it was I did not know for sure, but I hoped to discover it in this new world, the world of civilization. I sank into apathy. No doubt I felt lonely and wanted to see Button, my strange countryman, again.

One day I packed my saddlebags, rented a horse, and left for the school in the country.

I didn't like Button's general aspect. He was changed, thinner and pensive. He had either lost or was covering up the communicative quality which was so characteristic of him and he had sealed himself in a stony silence I couldn't break. Something drew my attention: he spoke very softly, almost in whispers. They had taught him how to ride, but he did not like horses—whereas the dogs followed him everywhere.

We walked aimlessly in the countryside which stretched as far as the horizon in gently rolling green hills. We were in spring and there was a radiance in the air that seemed marvelous after London. Toward late afternoon the sky clouded over and heavy rain broke loose; I had to beg him several times to go back to the house. The farmer's wife had prepared tea for us, and we took it to Button's room. Nothing seemed more pathetic to me than the sight of that room whose decent appearance could not hide its poverty. An iron bed, a chair, and a table with a pitcher, that was all. The ceiling, affixed to the granary's wall, slanted down to the eaves, where the water drained off. Its one narrow window faced the fields and let in a darkish grey light that shed a cloudy brightness on the room and our faces. Outside, about a hundred metres away on the slope, the wet English countryside began to roll away with the dark patches of woods. One on each side of the window, we stood quietly watching the rain.

"Wulaia, Jack. Tierra del Fuego."

His voice startled me.

"Father, mother, brothers." Button looked at me. I stood up straight.

"I understand. I also want to go back."

"When?"

"I don't know. The Captain is worried about it, he's working on it. I'm sure it will be soon."

I wanted to say something to lift his spirits, but I also felt trapped by the humdrum afternoon and didn't know what to say. At lunch the farmer's wife had said how amazed she was at the compassion aroused in Button by the sick. This had occurred at winter's end when the owner of the house had fallen ill with pneumonia. Button had looked after him devotedly, staying up night after night watching over his sleep.

"The lady says that you feel very sorry for sick people; are you going to be a doctor, Jemmy?"

I immediately regretted it. It was a stupid question. I had treated him like a child, or worse, like a backward person in whom we discover a unexpected skill.

"Doctor," he laughed openly for the first time. "Never doctor, Jack."

There was more truth in this sixteen- or seventeen-year-old than in any I had run into in all of London. I could know little of what he was going through, but that little moved me. I had to win back his confidence, which was no longer the same one that had united us during the passage and had dragged us along the streets of London during the first weeks.

"In Wulaia, all take care of sick people. It's the teachings, Jack."

"The teachings?"

"Yes. Teachings of the ancients. Which are your teachings?"

I was at a loss. Maybe Button had misconstrued my words. I thought it over but I had never had any ancients near me. Besides, talking to Button about the things Mallory had taught me would make no sense.

"I learned to break in horses, to herd them, to hunt otters, to steer a ship…"

Button kept shaking his head, he was beginning to show his old smile.

"Guevara don't understand, he has to learn."

Then he ran on about the very poor impression I had made on him during his first days on board ship and how he had been "very polite and patient" with me.

I was surprised and even offended. Uneasy because I had been an object of observation and hadn't even known it. But Button's glance was once more so friendly that I let out a big laugh.

"So I didn't make a big impression. You should have seen me peeling potatoes or scrubbing the deck…"

"What are your teachings?" Button insisted.

A little annoyed, I retorted: "What are yours, I'd like to know."

He was silent for a moment. He looked me in the eye. He was thinking over a decision it was difficult for him to make. He finally spoke.

"I tell you just a few, Jack. It is something they teach you in a secret place of the forest or the island, in the big wigwam, and it never leaves there. Three years ago I entered the big wigwam. In the *ciexaus,* very young women and men learn: the body fasts many days, the head has power over the body. Resistance, obedience. Education…is hard," for a few seconds he searched for the right word. "Severe, very severe. Is big secret, but Jack is my friend."

He put out his hands and took hold of my forearms above the wrists. I quickly did the same thing.

"Omoy-lume," he said.

"Omoy-lume?"

"Jemmy Button, no. Omoy-lume is my name."

Then he squatted like in his country. The rain's steady hum enveloped us; the grey afternoon light faded till it went out and transformed him into a silhouette without a face.

"After days of testing the body, when the night covers the sky and there is silence in the mountains and in the water, *uswaala kinana,* the great ancient teacher, gives a signal; young people sitting in circle listen: Most of all we, men and women, must be good and useful to the community. Each man and each woman must have power over himself or herself," Button's voice deliberately took on a solemn tone; he was concentrating as much as possible so that words would not fail him. "Learn to give up all excess. Each and every one of us, man or woman, must show greatest respect for old people. Old people know how to build the wigwam and the canoe, how to fight against the whale, they will help you to live, will console you, will tell you about ancestors. When any man insults you, don't do anything, talk alone with the one who offended you when you both calm down. Think: others have feelings just like you. Help orphans, take food to the sick, take care of strangers first. When you catch a big fish, you must share it; keep the smaller part. Children belong to everyone, look after them, help them, never punish them: you were once a child. When you marry, help your wife. Take care of the water; the trees, the fishes, and the animals belong to everyone. Don't kill just to kill. Light the fire at night to keep you warm and don't let it die."

He stopped.

"This not for white men," he said in the darkness. "From a long time ago, the teachings also talk about the whites. My father and other men talked about the things the white man used to do; when the whites came back, my countrymen took vengeance. The teachings about whites say we must fear them and keep away because they come to steal and rape women and little girls that are not yet women. They say that they kill, they butcher herds of seals, babies and mothers; they destroy everything. Intruders do not know nature. Last word of my father and other fathers and the ancients: the evil whites must not settle here in our land."

We were suspended in silence and in the dark. The window's dim rectangle was merely a grey patch that was fading out. It had stopped raining and outdoors the dogs were barking. From somewhere there came the unmistakable smell of food. The sense of an enormous error, of a violent distortion that had been committed and was still going on floated there, in the dark or within me, I don't know, and then disappeared. Seated on the floor in front of Button with my back against the wall, not knowing what to say, I lit my pipe.

Now, with the years, I can understand that moment: in a way that neither of us, being still very young, could wholly take in, Button was passing on a message. The impossibility of putting it clearly into words at the time did not make it less real. As I matured, in later encounters with Button—till the final meeting—this first impression deepened into certainty.

That afternoon our friendship was re-established and was sealed like a pact.

York, as always, went on being distrustful and morose. Fuegia, on the other hand, had a happy disposition and had cheerfully learned an astonishing number of tasks. I was surprised at how well they spoke English.

I was present at the classes their teacher gave them. One afternoon we sat through the visit—one of many, as I learned afterwards—of a married couple of landed gentry whose country house could be seen from the top of the hill. Among the titled persons in the neighborhood, coming to see the Yámanas was considered an exotic pastime and even fashionable. Poor Fuegia was the principal centre of attention; she had to perform all the charming things she knew. Every few minutes, the visiting lady, who sounded like a parrot, would remark:

"Wait till we tell the Captain about this! Wait till we tell this in London!" And glancing at her husband, she repeated, "We must show them off at home!"

Button did a demonstration of how to shoe a horse, and he had to recite The Lord's Prayer. The teacher was satisfied. The farmer's wife followed the performances complacently, with her clasped hands on her apron. When they insisted that Fuegia serve tea and name each of the items of the service, I interrupted. I said that I was following strict orders from the Captain to give them a private lesson, and that it was now the time for it.

I said goodbye three weeks later, promising that I would soon return with news from the Captain about the voyage. I rushed off at full speed, as if in London something urgent or decisive awaited me, and arrived at daybreak in a ghostly city covered with fog from the Thames. I immediately lost interest in it. I was full of confused feelings. Overcome by a general loathing, I did not leave my room at the inn on this or the following days.

The Captain sent for me, and I was a guest in his home for a few days. He knew about my trip to the farm and wanted to find out how the Yámanas were doing. It was odd seeing the Captain living on land. He was dealing with men who came from London and he was preoccupied with political matters about which, I realized, he was extraordinarily sensitive, especially because of his dignity and his noble blood, which always must be taken into consideration, above all, whenever a decision had to be made. Things did not turn out the way he hoped. He was definitely a man of the sea, and business deals on land presented other obstacles. They were impersonal and difficult. Men went about concerned only with their own affairs and not with something unique and substantial, like keeping a ship afloat.

That summer something occurred that was printed in the newspapers. The King and Queen expressed their wish to meet York, Fuegia, and Button. Proud, but always a little tense, the Captain had them fitted out in full regalia and we set out. Not having been invited to go in, I stayed in the carriage outside the entrance to St. James's Palace. However, Mr. MacDowell or MacDowness, all this pomp and circumstance did not hide a question for which there was no answer and which the people at the farm had no doubt already posed to the Captain: what was to be done with the Yámanas? Would they enter service in some home? Would their education continue? And if so, who would take care of expenses?

A cloud of uncertainty started to close in on those strange beings. They had appeared in the newspapers, gifts had been lavished on them, but this did not change things essentially. They had become embarrassing charges, around whom the germ of a distressing idea was beginning to grow and was gradually poisoning everyone from the Captain down to the last inhabitant of the kingdom who knew of their existence: what had they been doing there for over a year now? What had been the purpose of bringing them? The people in London were beginning to grow less and less interested in those strange savage inhabitants from no one really knew where, except that it was a hostile place abandoned by the hand of God, where the violence of the elements could attract none but the self-sacrificing souls of missionaries.

The Captain then made up his mind to fit out a ship with everything necessary for the return to Tierra del Fuego. He would do it out of his own pocket. He took me to the waterfront to see it. It was not a great ship, I must admit, but it would be good enough, if one gave no thought to the storms at the Cape. Nevertheless, our preparations restored my enthusiasm. Of late, I had hung around the waterfront too much. I would sit anywhere to watch the billowing sails gliding downstream to the sea.

And then one day the news that was to hasten everything arrived. Summoned urgently to the Admiralty, the Captain was once more granted the command of our ship and a scientific mission of great importance —to map the coasts of Brazil and Patagonia and study their flora and fauna. All expenses paid. As you no doubt know, Mr. MacDowell or MacDowness, the political designs that were recommending outposts in the extreme south of the American continent and the subsequent takeover of the Islands were behind these scientific expeditions. In any case, the Captain was exultant. He was, first of all, a career man who would be sure to carry out confidential instructions to the letter.

# FOLIO FIVE

Passing over the obvious fact that the Admiralty's abrupt shift in opinion was not the product only of a love of science or altruism but of the strategic value the Strait of Magellan and Cape Horn had acquired, the Captain displayed unusually fine humor, as if he had been infected by the general impatience reigning on board to weigh anchor, hoist sail, and return to sea.

As for me, I would soon be twenty years old and felt sure on my feet. One freezing November morning I arrived at the port with my bag on my shoulder. With bated breath I stood a long while looking at the ship, the same in which I had come to England more than a year ago: the men's shouts, the pounding of hammers, the snap of sails in the vibrant air all sounded to me like a familiar sea ditty, urging me to lose no time in boarding the ship again. The words Mallory had said to me such a long time before came back to memory: *A ship is like home.* I went up the gangplank in two strides.

Once on board, reality was less poetic. For this voyage I had been assigned a new task: to assist the boatswain with the ship's general accounts and the distribution of its stores. Button, Fuegia, and York seemed exhilarated by the return to their country and had abandoned their timidity. Their English was fluent, and they had no difficulty communicating, and not only with a crew of rough seagoing men. Their personal bearing at the royal palace had been admired by the nobility. The London public and the whole country had been touched by their departure. The press had said that England had a mission: to preach the gospel and to educate. Hadn't gifts come from all parts of the kingdom for the Fuegians Great Britain had taken in and educated and was now returning to their remote savage land to spread civilization and propagate the language? And hadn't these gifts—tea sets, table linens, knives, kitchenware for Fuegia and her home with York Minster—demonstrated the close ties between the English and their colonies, didn't they show the brotherly interest of the ordinary citizen for these poor souls? This is what the press said. As for the presents, Fuegia was the most enthusiastic about those gifts that, in any case, the Captain had given orders to pack and stow away in the hold. They would see them again in Cape Horn.

A few days after departure the Captain gave a kind of speech on the foredeck. He explained that the voyage was based on a scientific proposal which would benefit world navigation. Spanish cartography was much too deficient, he declared: defective and seldom precise, without taking into account the fact that large tracts of the coast of Patagonia and Tierra del Fuego had never been known until now. Our mission would make it possible for future navigators to stay afloat in those regions. I was enthusiastic about the Captain's speech and I believe the same may be said of all except the Yámanas, who remained indifferent. Later during lunch, the Captain was talkative as I had seldom seen him, or would see him afterwards. He even spoke about his first passage at the age of twelve.

It was soon evident that he had the same arbitrary and irascible character as always. In the morning we would see him appear on deck with a frown and the ice-cold eyes we all knew, looking for some corner of the ship that wasn't clean or shipshape. I often ate with him. He would question me about my tasks or the Bible, a subject in which I failed miserably, and this gave him the chance to also practice religious conversion on me. I think this was one of his motives for inviting me to his table.

But the time has come to introduce another member of our expedition, Mr. MacDowell or MacDowness, a man with whom we shared the long years of this voyage that would not end in Tierra del Fuego, and whom I never saw again after our return to England.

The day before our departure, a carriage pulled up its horses with a noisy flourish, almost on top of the gangplank, and two men got out. One was fairly old with a serious demeanor; he was wearing a black suit. The other was young, not very tall, in formal though not elegant dress, with a round face and lively manners.* They looked up at the deck. The older man shouted:

"Seaman! Here is someone who has to see the Captain!"

They went up the gangway.

Our passage to Tierra del Fuego had just been joined by a scholarly young man who had won the position of scientist on board, in response to an advertisement placed in the *Times* and on the strength of his excellent recommendations before the Admiralty. This was what the Captain said when he formally introduced him at dinner that evening. And he repeated the words of the mentor who had come with him to our ship: "A young scientist twenty-two years old, extremely intelligent, serious, and qualified," whom his professors had not hesitated to recommend warmly.

He brought along considerable luggage, and I helped him to make himself comfortable on board. An infinite number of objects came out of his satchel: measuring instruments, compasses, a small scale, magnifying glasses, pincers, a botanical and a geological catalogue, and a box packed with small vials labeled with Latin names. He had removed his hat and jacket and was doing the same thing I did with each of his possessions: he observed each item with the curiosity of a cat. His thoughtful, quiet eye became as sharp as a needle as soon as something caught his interest. This change began

---

* Guevara no doubt refers to Charles Darwin (Editor's note).

in his face and quickly absorbed his whole body; it was a general change in attitude, as on windy clouded days when the sea turns metallic and shifts from dark to light. If I tarry on this point, it is because that trait marked him; it was the most striking thing about his person and gave him a singular magnetism. In everything else, he seemed a perfectly normal young man like me, though with my six feet and some inches, I was half a head taller.

I was happy to discover his general good humor, which, from the first, eliminated any reservation between us. The qualification of "serious young man" was only a formal part of his recommendation. What was unquestionable was his scientific ability which he, as a matter of fact, put to the test on me. My wanderings through London's taverns had left me two things: a scar on my left arm and an embarrassing disease that tormented me in those days. The young doctor had studied medicine for a few years and had astonishing skills in botany. I don't know which of these he turned his hand to, but he ended up curing me of something that, he murmured discreetly, had not been at all infrequent among his fellow students.

From then on I named him the little doctor or Doc. On his part, he called me *gaucho*. He used to make fun of me and would add: the gaucho scholar. He tested me by throwing book titles and quotes from authors at me.

"There is something odd in this," he would comment, acting intrigued.

I treated him to my entire repertory, quoting excerpts and verses from here and there. I had never felt that what I had inherited from Mallory was a special privilege. Mallory himself had not given it more than a purely individual or perhaps filial value. So the boy I was would try to attract notice like someone parading well-developed biceps. What the books truly signified in my life, Mr. MacDowell or MacDowness, is something I kept to myself.

"What?" he would say to me, looking incredulous, "Do

gauchos know how to read? How is this miracle possible, if they're savages?"

I laughed, but it stung me in a way.

His interest in everything was inexhaustible. He would ask me what the pampa was like, what the Indians who lived there were like, what about the emus, and on and on about who the gaucho was and what he was like. There was a kind of exotic aura about him, which was praised by travellers who were intrigued by someone who could not be wholly pinned down as either savage or civilized man.

It was soon clear that the doctor was not much of a believer. This provoked head-on clashes with the Captain who, moreover, shared his cabin with him, since there were few creature comforts available on board. The two had rival characters and intellects. The naturalist—for this was the title the Captain had announced in the newspaper—was open and sharp; the Captain, touchy and closed. The doctor had a calm, humorous character; the Captain, the opposite. On two occasions—those I remember best—the discussion grew heated and the doctor left his berth, grateful, I am sure, that things had gone that far. At times he must have found the Captain's courtesy uncomfortable.

We are now in December, Mr. MacDowell or MacDowness. The days are long and the heat is constant. The nights, serene, swarming with crickets and stars. In the past two weeks I've written incessantly; yesterday, because of an inner need for contact with other people, I saddled my horse and went to the store. I stayed there all afternoon, catching up on neighborhood gossip and having a few drinks, deliberately delaying my return because of my recently discovered impatience with the fact that paper and ink were waiting for me here and also the memory of Button and the voyage that had not been like others. I mean for us who were part of it. A passage that for various reasons I am convinced was stamped on the memory of each of us and, one way or another, changed our lives.

When I got back home, I searched my trunk for the outlandish book by Lavater which the Captain had given me one night, and which my memory of the doctor has dragged to the surface now, such a long time afterward.

In the evening Graciana and I are having dinner in the gallery. She wants to know what I'm writing, and I explain without dispelling her bewilderment. Graciana is a gentle girl with lovely Creole features. She wears her hair gathered into two braids, and I've discovered that I like to watch her skillfully carry out this modest morning weave, without a mirror, looking into space with an absent air. Several days ago, with my arm and shoulder numb from exhaustion, I put aside my papers and went out into the gallery. When I came in again, she had lit the kerosene lamp. In the flickering light, without being aware that I was watching her, she had taken up the pen and was dipping it very carefully into the ink. If she hadn't seen me, I believe she would have tried to trace some letter.

I laughed heartily and offended her very much. I don't know if I've mentioned that the girl is illiterate. She went out into the patio and did not reappear till it was time to serve dinner, which she delayed till almost midnight.

As I wrote two days ago, remembering the doctor led me to look for the book I now have on the table.

A fitting example of the Captain's temperament once he became obsessed with an idea was his fancy for the theories about physiognomy held by a Frenchman, Kaspar Lavater, which he would enthusiastically describe in detail. The Captain was sure that a man's face, his physiognomy, revealed without any possible error his character and his inclinations. This brought on the first discussion between him and the

doctor during the passage, and for each this left the temperament and opinions of the other very clear.

We had been under way about two weeks, and they were
now friendly enough for the Captain to confess to him one
day at dinner that when he first saw Darwin, his nose had not
inspired the least confidence in him, and that if Darwin had
not come so well recommended by his professors at Cam-
bridge, the shape of his nasal appendage—that's how he put
it—would have been reason enough to reject him for the post.

Astonished but smiling, the doctor dropped his knife and
fork.

"What does my nose have to do with the position of
scientist on board, Captain?"

Satisfied to have drawn the attention of someone for
whom he was beginning to feel respect, the Captain launched
into a long and detailed explanation of Lavater's theory of
the laws of physiognomy. He pointed to the shelf where he
kept those books, asked me to get them, and set them down
on the table. One of these, the Italian translation, was the
book he gave me later, and which I now have in front of me.

Throughout the exposition, the doctor had shaken his
head several times, denying or at least casting doubt on what
he was hearing. With his incapacity to accept disagreement
from anyone else, the Captain ended his lecture by again
insisting on his theory about the nose. He remarked that the
minute he saw it he had begun to suspect that this nose did
not augur a good result for his scientific work. It was rather
puffy and ill-defined in shape, and in a way suggested someone erratic and weak-willed. He spoke as if he were referring
to a statue. Conditions, he said, that were in no way advisable
for a long voyage of scientific investigation, which required
firmness and character above all.

More and more surprised, the doctor answered:

"I hope you will allow me time enough to demonstrate
the contrary, Captain. On the other hand, you have called
that fellow Lavater a *scientist.*

The Captain:

"Absolutely. With a good number of irrefutable examples."

"Allow me to tell you, sir, that I consider *Monsieur* Lavater a vulgar quack."

For a few seconds all we could hear was the lapping of the water against the side of the ship.

"That's a little strong," the Captain replied. He had laid his knife and fork on his plate and was looking at him intently. "I repeat that he is very scientific. Absolutely scientific. All his opinions are illustrated; there is not one feature that is not exemplified and detailed."

"Scientific." Like an overhanging ledge above the doctor's eyes, the prominent space between them had become a frown. "Allow me to laugh, without offending you."

"What is so amusing about all this, sir?" the Captain said, without emotion.

The doctor took one of the volumes, the thickest one, and quickly flipped the pages. The captain was watching him seriously.

"I'll show you without much effort. Here, at random. Here Lavater explains what he means by 'physiognomic sensation.' Well, this thing about sensation..." The doctor shook his head as if he were thinking out loud. He read what I am reading here: "'By physiognomic sensation I mean those sentiments that are produced when we confront certain physiognomies and the conjectures which are inferred from them regarding those qualities of the mind produced by what is seen in such faces, or in their sketched or painted portraits...' Should I go on?"

"You choose at random, and this way everything is misconstrued. I insist that he's a man of science who has tirelessly studied human nature..."

"What he has studied are noses," the doctor broke in confidently; he appeared to be very comfortable with this type of discussion from which all consideration of rank between the speakers was removed. With the Captain, it was not the same. "Sensations, conjectures, sentiments... What are such words? Science is based on rigor and method. Only after classifying thousands of specimen and observing their singular and their common characteristics, is one in a position even to frame a mere hypothesis. What observations did this scientist make? How many thousands of faces did he classify? Of what races? Black, yellow...? Please, Captain..." Here he checked himself, sparks flying from his eyes. "Guevara!" he shouted. In the cabin's narrow space he and I were practically elbow to elbow, but this didn't stop me from jumping. "Please bring the savage here at once...!"

Hurt to the quick in one of his beliefs and favorite positions from which he usually classified men, the Captain had retreated behind his customary icy shell. I brought Button down from the deck as fast as I could, and there the four of us were.

Unmoved, smiling slightly, Button remained on his feet. Accustomed to being the centre of incomprehensible scenes between whites, he accepted them patiently.

"Look at this face!" The doctor continued his argument, addressing the Captain. "What do you see in this nose? What does this nose, compared to mine, clarify? Is it broader, longer, flatter, fleshier, more pointed...?" With his nervous fingers he had taken hold of Button's cheeks and was switching his face from side to side to demonstrate better what he was saying. "And his jutting brow, something like mine...? And these prominent cheekbones and this cunning smile?" Button stopped smiling. His eyes darkened and became fixed on an angle of the cabin a few inches above our heads. "What do you say? What distinctions or, rather, what categories of distinctions between the somatic and cranial characteristics can you establish between two different races so that two centimeters more width or two more of narrowness will result in similar or different character? What nose length do you consider equivalent? And from this what general conclusions can you draw? If it is not universal, it is not scientific, sir. We have to discover laws. Universal laws, not analogies..."

As if turned to stone, the Captain was staring at the doctor. I was staring at the Captain, also petrified. Button was inscrutable, looking at the sea through the cabin's porthole. The Captain was wearing a shirt and a vest, but he seemed to be in uniform with his badges and medals; the doctor, on the other hand, had become boyish. His flushed round face and his nervous movements made him look like a boy. But in spite of his excitement, his tongue was razor-sharp and his mind remained as cold as a gravestone. The Captain was just the opposite: hard on the outside, his arguments and even his eloquence yielded before the fire of the indignation burning inside him. As I watched them, I was learning something about men.

"Allow me!" The doctor, who could no longer be stopped, went on. He picked up one of the volumes, this one I rescued from my trunk and have with me now. He was wetting his finger with his tongue and turning the pages. "Two editions. The English translation and the abridged Italian: *Il Lavater portabile*. I didn't know you read Italian, Captain. Here it is. Listen to this: *Il naso,* it's what concerns me, *il naso*. I judge that, according to you, this is the part that has to do with me... how about this illustration?" He spun the book around and—before our faces, including Button's—he passed around the sketch of a rather fleshy nose. *"Un naso sensa veruna inflesione decisa, e simile a una informe massa di carne, non será mai propio d'un uomo di genio strordinario.* 'A nose with no decisive inflection, similar to a shapeless mass of flesh, will never be that of a man of extraordinary genius.' What does decisive inflection mean? That the *mass* of flesh is not decidedly bent to one side or the other, that it doesn't curve downward and just hangs there, that it doesn't turn upward? And the other thing; perhaps it doesn't correspond to an "extraordinary genius" but only to "a little talent" or "almost no talent"? What kind of terms are these, sir? Are these scientific terms?"

"You surprise me, sir," the Captain said in a cutting tone. "Science seems to be your God, an excessively practical and materialistic God, much too fallible..."

"God? What does God have to do with this conversation, sir?"

"Well, we could admit the hypothesis, if you like, sir, although your scientific pride stops you from regarding the Almighty as the machine and prime mover of all Creation."

"Hypothesis! Pardon me, Captain, but there are certain subjects that touch me deeply... We were talking about something else. God is the ace up the sleeve of illogic. But since you insist, sir, let's make that hypothesis part of this after-dinner conversation. Why not!" He was turning the pages of the book so hard that I thought he would pull it apart. "Let's see!" He pointed out sketches that represented all kinds of heads, noses, ears. "Let's take a look here. If what I understand of your physiognomic theory is correct, we would have material examples of evil and good correspond to the shape of a pear. All in all, the evil and the good which the Almighty has cast out to fly over the world are embodied *sub specie* of noses and the crowns of people's heads. Here we have a different example: *L'imbecilitá...* Why has divine power distributed something in such an arbitrary way? Why should a human being, at the very moment he is being created...?"

"Careful, sir, you are moving dangerously close to blasphemy."

The doctor seemed to be alone in the cabin. Button had an enigmatic smile on his face. I remember that I was delighted.

"...at the very moment he is being created a human already carries in his features his destiny of good or cruelty, of genius or imbecility! Is it just? I ask you. Does this seem a noble Divine plan? Is this a just God? Don't your two beliefs contradict each other?"

"Certainly not, sir," the Captain said, from the fortress of his shell. "Certainly not. You yourself are the proof. Your nose is not the most adequate for the job, according to the theory I hold. Too round and fleshy and right now, I must add, if you'll excuse me, red and blotchy like an unredeemed drunkard's. Such as you've had the kindness to read a moment ago. And yet, I fervently believe in the power of the human will whereby God lets us see a spark of his infinite light. I believe in the will that, with enormous effort can rectify a man's natural affinity for indecision, laziness, or vice, and can lift the soul toward..."

"You confuse me with those arguments, sir!" the doctor broke in with disrespect. "Who is in command in human nature then: the low standard of form, the flesh, pure materiality, or the spirit? Apparently for your scientific book it's the first of these. Observe this, look at this simian face, sir." In the book he picked out a truly monstrous face which Button and I leaned over to see. "God denies this, one of His creatures, a soul, abandons it... How do you explain this, sir? This gentleman will be condemned to apehood, to imbecility for all eternity, or will God do him the favor of throwing him a spark?"

"Undoubtedly, sir, when your recommendations for this position were reviewed, religious beliefs were not examined."

"God put in the spoon and stirred, and there's nothing more to be said," the doctor continued on his own. "All arguments are subject to the judgment of that power, which is unlimited and omnipotent, beyond any scientific discussion."

"You are trying nothing less than to keep God out of this matter, sir!" The Captain shouted, losing control.

"That's right, sir!" The other shouted in turn.

"In that case, I can't go on speaking with you, sir!"

"It's not necessary, sir. I'm leaving right now."

He started hastily stuffing papers, books, and clothing into a bag.

Button and I slipped out behind him.

A couple of hours later the doctor was in the prow calmly talking to the boatswain about the stars, no doubt asking him something about the constellations. The strong wind blowing was ruffling his thinning straight hair and had evidently swept far away the heated discussion in the cabin. The doctor was precisely the opposite of a resentful man.

To be honest, before going on there's something I must say. There are vivid memories that remain perfectly clear in my mind: almost all are related to Button, Isabella, and Mallory's friend; and there are others that I reconstruct, like these arguments between the Captain and the young doctor. Though not exact, for some reason they have stuck in my memory, and I lend them words to let them recover part of their truth. No doubt every one of those who were in that cabin would give a different version than mine. As my excuse, I can say that this is my story and it obeys the only thing that naturally dominates it: my memory.

The Captain let two days go by before again inviting Darwin to share his cabin. At the same time, Button was able to get even.

The young doctor did not bear up well at sea—he suffered *mal de mer*—and the rollers made him ill. Yellow in the face, where the unattractive nose disapproved of by the Captain stood out more than ever, he sat on a bench on deck, unable to move or do anything. Then Button came over to him and said, full of sympathy:

"Poor fellow! You poor, poor fellow!" and tapped him gently on the back. Then he went off without even hiding the smile that two steps later turned into hearty laughter. To Button, who had spent his life in a rocky canoe, seeing a grown man get seasick was very funny.

We had left the coast of Brazil behind some days before and were heading down toward Montevideo. During the hours we shared in the cabin, we talked about Button, his progress with English, about books and nautical themes in general, but on this day the conversation took another turn. While preparing to shave, the Captain offered us a solemn and well-grounded defense of slavery, a system prevalent in Brazil's plantations. In the middle of the Captain's talk—he was carefully honing his razor—the doctor interrupted him and for his part began a diatribe against slavers and plantations.

"It's something infamous for the human species, sir. And, I must add, I am astonished that you should defend it."

The Captain paused in the act of sharpening his razor and said with a half-smile:

"Let me tell you something that I am sure will interest you: in my presence, by way of demonstration, Senhor Dos Santos Leyva, one of the most prominent planters in Brazil, had all his slaves, a big crowd of adults and children, assemble in the yard of his *fazenda*. From the porch of his magnificent house, where we were, he asked them in a loud voice if they were happy, to which the slaves replied in chorus: "Yes!" And then he also asked them if they wanted to be free. And adults and children, again in chorus, answered with a loud and clear "No!" What do you think of that? You see, sir, it wasn't told to me; I was there."

Satisfied with himself, the Captain watched the face of the other man, whose cheeks were burning.

"And do you believe," the doctor said softly, "that if their master had not been there the answer would have been the same?"

Caught off-balance in the firm belief in his argument, which had seemed airtight to him since he was talking about facts, it was now the Captain's turn to blush. His surprise made him spring to his feet. Fortunately, since his early youth his body was well used to the height of the cabin's ceiling or else he would have broken his neck. He threw the shaving cup full of soapy water on the floor, without even apparent notice.

"As usual you don't know how to measure your words, sir," the Captain said.

"I don't think I have said anything offensive, sir, except about slavery."

"If you will allow me, I should like to shave alone, sir."

The doctor was already announcing that he was going to sleep in the hold, in the seamen's bunks, and was picking up armfuls of papers and books, and making his way down the passageway to the hatch.

That same night I was asked to take him a note of apology from the Captain who once more invited him to share his cabin, where at least he had the minimum convenience of a table where he could work on his notes.

What I have just related will help to explain what drove the Captain to his adventure with the Yámanas, which corresponds perhaps with the most inflexible part of his way of thinking. If he truly believed that slaves were happy, he might very well take a Yámana away from his homeland and undertake the experiment of civilizing him.


I know that this is not the whole truth, Mr. MacDowell or MacDowness. Reality is more complex, and surely my art of writing is not enough to sketch in the finer shades of the Captain's interest—if we may call it that—in Button, which unexpectedly involves his place in England's political power scheme and, it cannot be denied, his humanitarian and religious side. Ripening within him, perhaps, was the suspicion that the Admiralty's men placed no trust in him, in his political capacity—though they definitely did in his capacity as seaman, which was unquestionable—and perhaps he was trying to demonstrate something.

Cape Horn received us with a storm. According to the Captain, it was the roughest storm he had had to weather since he first set foot on a ship. Today I can say the same thing.

Leaving the Strait of Le Maire, rounding the Cape of Good Success, I believe the Captain, for the only time in his life, acted against his professional common sense. Something was making him anxious to leave the Yámanas in their country, to see what point the civilizing experience had reached, to prove that his experiment had been a success. It was January, the worst time of year to cross the Horn westward. The ship was running the storm with a minimum of canvas. When the waves reached us—in the Antarctic sea the waves come in runs of three, one after the other, like mountains closing in on the ship—, our small vessel, charging along, rose on the first crest which slowed down its advance. The second stopped her dead and put us broadside to the storm, and the third hit her sideways and dropped her onto the sea. As we mariners say, Mr. MacDowell or MacDowness, "the ship fell asleep." There's a terrible moment of panic because if she doesn't come out of it, if she turns over completely, there is no saving her, it's certain death for all. Happily, the ship recovered her vertical position, and the masts once more pointed to the dark threatening sky, and we men were able to hug one another, terrified but safe and sound. The only loss was a boat which was pulled "by the roots" from its supports and flew off into the storm.

Button's always irascible gods, now turned loose, were defying us. Perhaps we had transgressed the very foundations of that world—untouched and motionless in time—and nothing would ever be the same again.

At midnight on that terrible day, we were able to anchor in treacherous Cape Horn. A few days later we went ashore in Wulaia, Jemmy Button's country. As I have said, it was

January, the middle of summer, a season of unrivaled beauty in Tierra del Fuego.

At our feet the boat nibbled at the pebbles of the beach with a hollow sound. Button and I were studying the bay. Quiet as a pond, it opened in a semicircle amidst a calm of incomparable majesty. A river of ice flowed into it. The small capricious forms of the ice-floes moved away imperceptibly from the main pack to founder on the rocky salients of the shore. Every now and then in the impressive silence we could hear the dry report of breaking ice, which rose with repeated echoes toward the mountains of perpetual snow. Behind us a stretch of coarse sand, crisscrossed with roots, was covered with leaves and lichens of a blackish green colour. Gloomy and dank, humming with low sounds, sudden wing-beats, and calls that crossed from shore to shore, the forest began at the coast itself. The tree trunks gleamed, covered with moss of a deep emerald colour. The channel's turbulent waves slowed down as they entered the bay and died among the rocks with gentle thrusts that made the boat nibble at the beach.

Button stared intently into the distance straight ahead.

"Guanacos," he said.

Across the way, the coast of Navarino Island rose into view. A huge mass of clouds surrounded the peaks of the mountains on the island. Just a short while later I made out some tiny dots moving along the crest of a hill.

After that single word, Button had kept silent a long while.

Nor did I know how to express my anger at what he had gone through several days before, whose effect continued to weigh upon us, and I also opted for silence. There was nothing to say. That morning Button had wanted to show me the hidden bay of his childhood and it was like a friendly sign, a hospitable gesture, after the unsettling days that followed our arrival.

What had occurred was this. The Captain put Button ashore on his islands, completely dressed in English fashion, even to hat and gloves. An erroneous judgment had led him to believe that Button's clothes would cause a stir of admiration and curiosity among the Yámanas. No one ventured an opinion about this or contradicted it. Including me. A strange passivity had taken hold of Button. He stood quietly a few paces away from the beach, surrounded by the ship's crew, busy landing from the boats the boxes with everything they brought from England and pausing now and then to look at him. The strangeness of the situation did not escape these men. In the air there was something indefinable, like a scene at a carnival, which the Captain, curious and excited as he was, honestly appeared not to notice. Suddenly Jemmy looked up. An incredible way off he had recognized the sharp voice of his older brother whom we couldn't yet see. A moment later the canoes started to come into view in the bay. I was able to count forty approaching from all directions. A rush of alarm shook the sailors, who went for their weapons in the boats.

The Captain and the doctor had had a long talk about this encounter. How would Button behave? The Captain was dead certain that at least part of what had been learned in the civilized world would begin to work right away. The doctor doubted this. As for me, sitting on a rock some distance away, Button's double humiliation was a slap in my face.

Standing on the pebbles on the beach, knowing that he was being observed—dressed in full regalia, his boots pathetically well polished—, Button instinctively lifted his head to sniff the sea lions' sour smell.

The first canoes ran up the beach, and the others followed. Button met the one belonging to his family, walked a few steps in its direction and stopped. His mother, four brothers, and two sisters jumped into the water and pulled the canoes as far as the rocks. The expression on Button's face was a mixture of shame and fear, and the one moment when he managed to blurt out an incomplete English phrase, he lowered his head. I was just able to hear something he murmured in Spanish, something that sounded like: "Don't you know?" His people formed a circle around him. Men and women also got out of the other canoes; they were talking among themselves and reproaching us, their voices growing louder and louder. Then there was a grim silence. They steadily looked him up and down, without a word. His sisters seemed not to know him and ran back to their canoes, as if they were afraid of him. His mother made a complete turn around her son and also went back to her canoe, as if to make sure it was safely tied up. Later on we discovered that three years before, Jemmy's mother had looked for him desperately for months, believing that her son had escaped from the ship. Yet she displayed no feeling now and seemed neither happy nor sad. She just looked at her canoe, the focus of her concern.

"Speak to them," the Captain ordered. "Explain where you are coming from, what you are bringing them. Speak to them!"

Button was still painfully silent, with lowered head. Not a sound left his throat, as if the words wouldn't come, neither the English nor his own. He addressed no one in any language. No one spoke to him.

"Have you forgotten your language?" The Captain went to one of the cases and opened it roughly. "Show them what we brought from England, what civilization brings them! Speak up!"

Button slowly removed his hat without a word.

"Speak to them! I command you!" The Captain lost his imperturbable composure.

The Yámanas began to leave. They got into their canoes and nimbly headed for deep water, paddling faster and faster, moving away, disappearing behind the rocky headlands.

Jemmy's family did the same. At the last moment his older brother came to him. He spoke a few dry, sharp words.

They moved off.

The weight of those three years of uprootedness had come down hard on Button. He was probably as much ashamed of the nudity of his people as he was of his own regalia. The long years of living with the whites had partly erased from his mind the naked state in which his people lived and now he was ashamed.

We watched them disappear, paddling their canoes, with their children and their dogs, to light the night's fires. The bay was deserted; only the cormorants were once again gliding above the rocks. From the islets came the roar of the sea lions, which sounded like a funeral lament to me. We all remained motionless, as if waiting for something to happen. Carefully Jemmy placed the hat and gloves on a rock. A single broken sound emerged from his throat when he saw the last canoe disappear behind the sea lions' rocks.

The Captain turned his back on Button and broke the silence, which had brought us to a standstill like an evil spell, by giving the sailors forceful orders; they had to pile up the boxes and cover them in case it should rain, and the tents must be put up. We would spend those days on land, until we had built the house and left it ready for Jemmy, Fuegia, and York. The civilizing post which was Great Britain's dream.

I approached Button: "What did your brother tell you?"

I wasn't sure he wanted to talk but he did.

"My father died last winter."

This caught me completely off balance; I had imagined reproaches and accusations.

"I'm very sorry, Jemmy."

"I already knew. At the farm I dreamed my father dead. It's always that way."

As the doctor casually expressed it, that night during the dinner improvised in the tent put up on the beach, the meeting had been as interesting as that of two horses in the middle of a field. He was as triumphant before a beaten Captain as if there had been a sort of unspoken wager between them. I foresaw a long argument coming up concerning those "poor beings" whom the young doctor hardly considered human. I begged to be excused from dining with them and went out.

York and Fuegia were eating with the animated circle of seamen around the fire. They had gone fishing for shellfish and, as if doing this had all at once given them back their native land, they looked happy, their faces shining in the glow of the flames. There's nothing so beautiful as a windless summer night in Tierra del Fuego: the ship's lanterns glittered faintly on the water, the trees nearby, lit up by the fire, created strange fleeting apparitions and the smoke rose toward a sky where the peerless Southern Cross shone. Button and I watched it for a long while. A unique serenity came down from the mountains and, like a balm, seemed to rub away what had happened that afternoon. On the other side of the channel, in the blackness along the coast, the eternal bonfires of the Yámanas rose into the night.

But the quiet was only an illusion. What had taken place stuck to Button like a splinter driven into his flesh.


I must write that I cannot understand why the Captain's failure, the evidence of this failure, cheered me up. I had taken Button's part on the spur of the moment, but why? Our friendship apart, was it perhaps because I also suffered the Captain's proud authority and feared all it stood for? Was it perhaps because through Button I was taking my own vengeance on an England I both hated and loved? I don't know. Nor do I believe it's important to this story to look deep into the mixed feelings whose importance to me, if it existed, I no longer remember.

In any event, I felt possessed by an intense satisfaction I couldn't explain and which I had to conceal somehow. It wasn't based on what I saw in a taciturn Button who for longer and longer periods would vanish into the forest or the islands, into parts of his country that were unfamiliar or inaccessible to us.

I soon discovered that under his inscrutable exterior Jemmy was recovering his territory in great gulps—the wind and the forests, the sea, and the mountains—and that this was coupled with a joy that, like me, he had decided to conceal. It was then that one morning he told me he wanted to show me a hidden spot, a bay where he had spent a good part of his childhood.

And there we sat now—with the water gurgling at our feet—letting the night come down slowly, watching the flocks of petrels, rising and descending in brilliant harmony, race over the water's surface to catch insects.

We didn't move or talk, but Button was there in a different way than I was.

"Pálala," he said, startling me. I was half asleep. "Pálala!"

"What is that?" I said, half sitting up and resting my elbow on the sand.

"My people's word for your people," Button said. "Pálala: people nobody can understand. The white man's things have no use here. Ship very big but not good for fishing; house made of wood, no good against fire, boots slip on rocky ground..." He fell silent once more.

I was trying to explain to myself something that filled me with curiosity. In some mysterious way I didn't understand, Button had control over the natural world around him. Any other way, survival would have been impossible. His was a purely human tenacity which no doubt became intensified in times of misfortune and hostility, when the polar wind blew and the world was a gloomy place, immersed in a raging storm.

Mr. MacDowell or MacDowness, I had the strange feeling that he represented us, that there at the end of the continent, Button and his clan were lighting their bonfires and bearing witness to the presence of mankind. It may seem exaggerated but, as I have already noted somewhere, the only rules that hold for me are those of my own experience.

Something was evident: as he recovered his world, Button withdrew from us.


In a few days, the wooden house was erected and the vegetable garden marked off with a stone wall. It was a camp where, following the Captain's plan, Button would be left with everything brought from England, and where also, in his bucolic imagination, Fuegia and York and their children would make their home. I saw how senseless all this was. Thousands of miles away the idea had been acceptable and even praiseworthy, but when it materialized on the spot, it became absurd. Nature does not give imagination a chance. The seeds for an experimental vegetable garden had been carefully ordered and classified. The teakettles, bed clothes, tools, pots and pans, rakes, pitchers, knives—a modest synthesis of civilization's gifts—would be left there, under a cloudy sky in an unpredictable and savage climate.

Our ship continued its mission along the Pacific coast. One year later we would again pass through the Cape on our return to England. We would then see for ourselves the outcome of what the Captain had started almost four years before.


This afternoon, while Graciana silently went around preparing the maté, I went through my trunk again. I found what I sought, a copy of the *Times* of Saturday, December 10, 1859, which includes the letter of a particular reader who explains —perhaps better and no doubt more objectively than I—some doubtful aspects of the so-called Patagonian Mission. The signer of the letter is George Rennie, ex-Governor of the Islands.

This is what Rennie writes:

"At the end of March 1855 Captain Snow came into Port Stanley in a small schooner. When I received him with two of his group, they told me that they had been sailing in the western part of the Islands and had landed so that two members of the expedition might settle on Keppel Island with material to build houses and commercial establishments, and, from what I was able to find out, with a minimal supply of provisions.

"Like me, the Colonial Secretary, who was present, was very much concerned about the great rashness of such an action. I cannot recall the exact words I used, but I know that I mentioned to Captain Snow the advantage, indeed necessity, of urgently sending them supplies they would surely soon lack. Since we never received a reply to our suggestion, it would not be unlikely for Captain Snow to be charged with homicide if one or both of the men left on Keppel should die because of this deficiency."

I am interrupting this to bring up something, Mr. MacDowell or MacDowness, that you probably know: the said Captain Parker Snow was something like the advance guard of the Mission which, with great excitement and public inscription, was in the final stages of preparation in England. Its leader would be the Reverend Despard, shortly to depart with his family to take possession of the settlement on Keppel Island in the Falkland archipelago. Parker Snow was a Mission employee, a seaman. It soon became clear that he did not see eye-to-eye with his employers, the missionaries. Ex-Governor Rennie continues:

"Not desiring to place any obstacles in the way of this romantic enterprise, I immediately agreed to grant them the right of occupancy. Then the conversation shifted to the manner in which this business would be carried out. They said that Reverend Despard had not yet left England, and therefore, until his arrival, they would serve as pioneers. They would take the first steps toward the raising of cattle and would fetch the Fuegians who, while being instructed in Christianity, would be employed in various activities and tasks.

"I answered that the objective was highly laudable but I couldn't see its viability, and I asked them how they would manage to make the natives settle on the island. Captain Parker Snow and his friends looked at one another in confusion, and, after a pause, one of them said innocently: 'I suppose we shall buy them from their chiefs.'

"I warned them as severely as I could of the possibility of their being accused of kidnapping should they act that way and told them that if they brought those miserable savages to the Falkland Islands, it would be my duty to initiate an investigation to see whether they had come of their own free will, with legal contracts."

Ex-Governor Rennie laments that the Mission went ahead, and before ending he says: "Despite the success of Captain Snow and his men in persuading a number of Fuegians to go to Keppel Island, I cannot affirm that they are being provided with essentials." Then he concludes:

"I am not well-informed about what steps the missionaries followed after this, my tour of duty having ended and because of my return to England a short time later. I can't reproach myself for not having assumed responsibilities without taking adequate measures to prevent a repetition of a deplorable tragedy like that of Captain Gardiner."

This letter of apology by the ex-Governor of the Falkland Islands is indeed interesting. It shows the strictly legalistic character of the Empire's officials even in one of its remotest corners. This became evident at Button's trial, for which an investigation was set up that, with some exaggeration, might well be titled: The Empire against Jemmy Button.

One year later, after cruising up and down the Pacific coast, we returned to the Cape and went up as far as Wulaia where twelve months before we had built the small wooden house. As we approached Murray Strait, I was in the prow waiting to catch sight of Button's canoe and his silhouette as he came out to meet us. I believe the Captain hoped to see him together with York and Fuegia in the doorway or to surprise them, like good farmers, gathering potatoes in the garden.

Almost nothing was left of the house. Some pathetic vegetables had managed to spring up here and there and a wind like a hurricane was buffeting them mercilessly. The only thing left as a sign of our work was the stone wall around the lot where the house had been built. No one could ask for greater desolation. Ironically, the solitude was all the more striking because of the dance of the cormorants repeating their endless rise and fall in order to drop clams from the air to break on the rocks. I stood watching their ancestral motion, swinging up and down.

We walked along the empty cliffs pursued by the wind's noise, the Captain, without uttering a word, making observations and jotting them in his notebook, but I knew that what really mattered to him was finding Button to see what had happened. The doctor was collecting stone samples. The crew was looking for drinking water to fill the barrels. I climbed to the top of a hill. In the middle of the desolate landscape I shouted at the top of my lungs: Jemmy Button! No one appeared. Low clouds covered the summits, the hills along the channel's northern coastline looked black, and it began to drizzle. There were no fires warning of our presence nor smoke columns rising behind the cliffs in the familiar signal that we had been sighted. Where had they all gone? A sense of foreboding disheartened the eight men who had come ashore in the boats. When evening fell we returned to the ship. No one dared say what he was thinking: that possibly Button had died or perhaps, even worse, his own people had killed him. I said so to the Captain. A year had gone by and perhaps his countrymen had not pardoned him for his voyage with the white men.

"I don't think so," the Captain said tersely.

The doctor, on the other hand, thought everything was possible, anything might have occurred. Nothing logical could be expected from that human group.

I asked to stand the night watch and stayed on deck. There were no fires on the coast. Early the next morning we were having coffee in the Captain's cabin when we heard shouts on deck. I went up right away and looked over the ship's side, with the Captain behind me.

What we saw left us speechless. A canoe was approaching to starboard; a girl, almost a child, was skillfully stroking the water, first one side then the other, a small fire at her feet. Standing at the bow was a man. He was naked, skinny, with a mass of tangled hair. A sealskin not much bigger than a handkerchief around his shoulders was all that protected him from the wind. His face, painted black, was crossed by two parallel white lines, one even with his upper lip from ear to ear and the other above his eyelids from temple to temple. It was Jemmy Button. His aspect was scary, and it dawned on me that the paint, which I took for war-paint or for intimidation, transformed him and would arouse in an adversary—if he were a white man like me—the instinctive impulse of self-defense.

When I was able to recover myself, an involuntary cry rose from my throat.

"Button! Jemmy! Up here, up here."

Skillfully maneuvered, the canoe came alongside the ship. Then Button did something intended for the Captain and me. A gesture of deliberate or perhaps condescending courtesy. He bent down in the canoe, leaned over the water and with both hands washed his face and removed the paint from his neck and his body. He stood up again:

"Jack! Captain! I'm coming up."

We tossed him the ladder.

Standing on deck, Jemmy looked thin but more muscular than a year ago. He had changed, he was no longer a boy but a man with a powerful body, and he looked much stronger than I. Something I can't explain emanated from him, a self-assurance which showed in his presence alone, in the way he stood there on deck without moving. All of us greeted him with words only because Button kept a space between himself and us and apparently didn't want to come up close to shake hands.

There was, as never before, a great distance between him and the whites. This figure barely gave us a glimpse of the Button with English boots and jacket, the London Jemmy of a year ago. In the Captain's eyes, this man who had returned to the most primitive human state, gone back to what his ancestors had been, a nomadic canoe Indian, had kept nothing of what he had been given. He had done nothing. He hadn't played his part. He had civilized no one, had not handed on to his people anything he had learned. He was the image of his own failure.

In spite of the devastating effect this irrefutable fact had on the Captain, he recovered and invited him to share dinner with him and myself in his cabin. At least Jemmy still retained a lot of his English. In the doctor's opinion, Button's reversion to the savage state was not surprising in the least.

"Good to eat food. I need clothes," Button said with a glance at me.

I fetched him a pair of trousers and a seaman's blouse. A sad smile appeared on the Captain's lips when he saw that Jemmy used his knife and fork correctly and was recovering fluent English in conversation. Yet there was great tension in the air. Button regarded us from an unbridgeable distance. There was neither resentment nor happiness in his eyes, only distance. He told us he had married, that there had been incursions by sealers, and that a very hard winter was on the way. The Captain asked him about the house and about Fuegia and York. As if he were dealing with remote events from a time it was hard for him to remember, Button threaded together a brief account from which it was clear that as soon as the ship's stern was out of sight, the Yámanas hidden behind the hills had come out and carried off everything. In their land there still prevailed the ancient customs which perhaps he had forgotten in the country of the white men: anyone who has too much of anything must share it with his brothers. As for Fuegia and York, they had taken everything they owned, packed it in their canoe, and stolen off at night— while the others slept—to their own land. The house had been dismantled for the use of its lumber.

Button related what I now reconstruct, without batting an eye, with no emotion in his voice.

"Don't you wish to return to England, Jemmy?" The Captain had asked the question in a severe, perhaps recriminatory, tone.

A scream pierced the cabin's tense atmosphere, followed by other pitiful sharp wails. An impassive Jemmy explained that they were his the cries of his wife. The girl was hailing him from the canoe.

"Afraid the whites will take Button away."

He looked at us, expressionless. The cries were more and more heart-rending. No one budged, since Jemmy himself did not. We went on eating quietly. Suddenly he got to his feet. The Captain and I did the same. We went up on deck behind him. The poor skinny little creature, guarding her only possession, the canoe, stood screaming, her young breasts shaken by sobs and shudders. I noticed the swelling of her belly.

"Jemmy Button coming into canoe!" He insisted desperately in English.

Suddenly he leaned over the side and in Yámana yelled a few dry, sharp words. The girl calmed down as if by magic. Button faced us. He looked at the Captain as if he were resuming the conversation in the cabin.

"No more England, Captain. Never more England."

He started removing his clothes to return them. I told him to keep them. I hurried down to the hold, and wrapped together bread, biscuits, and whatever I found at hand for his wife. He stood back to receive it. In a second he was on the deck's rail ready to jump. I went to him.

"Goodbye, Jemmy," I said, going closer to embrace him.

His look stopped me in my tracks. A second later, the indefinable glimmer of irony or complicity reappeared deep in his eyes. He put out his hand.

"Goodbye, Jack."

Before the canoe drew away from the ship, Button showed me something, a gift for me: a harpoon made of bone, which he tossed skillfully up to my hands. The canoe left. The woman was paddling, and I admired the strength with which such a fragile creature moved away from us.

As a final gesture, Button lit a bonfire on the coast, which I took as a signal for me. The Captain, morose, had shut himself in his cabin. The doctor remarked that he was more interested in the rocks and lichens than in those savages.

Although I thought so at the time, that was not the last time I would see Jemmy.


Today I made a decision. These last few months, seeing Graciana so intrigued by my writing, which she cannot share, I have given her a task of her own. I have asked her to start sewing these sheets together as if they were pages. I've explained that it's the way books are made. She has taken this task so seriously and devotedly that I can't help being moved.

I don't think I've told you, Mr. MacDowell or MacDowness, that a few months before definitely returning to my country at the end of 1856 I passed through Cape Horn for the last time. In those years I was sailing on a Dutch ship, and I had told its captain Button's story. On this occasion, my familiarity with the area was a great help to the pilot, and this allowed me to ask the captain for something I wanted: to try and find Button, to go through the labyrinth of islands and channels of his country to find out if he were still alive. It was the first time the Dutch had navigated through the archipelago, and the legends of horror about its inhabitants, which circulated in the ports of Europe, did not predispose them to remain around there longer than strictly necessary. We were detained by a thick fog, and I asked the captain to let me use a boat to go ashore. This seemed like madness and, in part, it was. I was aware of this last opportunity, my last passage through Button's country. I did not ask anyone to go with me nor did anyone volunteer. I carried a bag with gifts for Jemmy and his family, in the unlikely event that I might run into them.

I finally stepped down and started to row. We were near the Murray Strait, at the mouth of Ponsonby Fjord, in the middle of Button's country. It was a place I remembered very well. Nevertheless, the fog made it phantasmagoric, ghostly and disquietingly unfamiliar to me. The mountains and hillsides had disappeared; all points of reference were vanishing into a milky brightness which enveloped in flurries and eddies everything that existed there.

I was beginning to think it had all been a crazy venture when on the port side, like a strange ghost, a small ice floe came at me, its shape so unusual that it startled me. For a moment I was paralyzed. I shipped the oars and stood up.

"Jemmy Button!"

My shout was lost in the mist; a faint echo came from far

away. I kept rowing slowly. I could hear wings flapping, water noises. I shouted again once or twice. I turned the boat around ready to retrace my way and return to the ship but I could no longer make out the lantern they had lit for me on the cross-tree of the mainmast. I could distinguish nothing except my knees. Ahead of me I lost my boat's bow in the thick cloud of fog. I thought I could see a white wall. I went through seconds of panic.

"Ja-mus Button, here!"

Before me, as if risen out of nothing, the black prow of a canoe came into view. Someone stood up in it.

"Button, here."

He made signs for me to follow his canoe. A young woman, a small boy some three years old, and a dog had come with him. Shortly afterwards we leapt ashore and pulled the boats onto the pebbles. I gave him a long hug which he received stiffly. His aspect was deplorable, in spite of which he was still imposing. The 18-year-old boy fascinated by a pair of gloves had been left very far behind; now he was a thickset middle-aged man like me. A man who watched me silently. He raised one hand and touched my arm.

"Jack."

"Friend," I said.

"Yes, Jack friend," Jemmy repeated with difficulty and seemed to expand. "Many years."

He pointed to his face and mine. I agreed:

"Many years, Jemmy."

He went into action at once. I don't know how but he had gathered some branches in the middle of the fog and now sent his wife to fetch embers from the canoe. In the next moment the fire lit up and warmed us. The woman sat down timidly, a little apart from us, with the child between her knees and the dog at her side. Jemmy crouched next to the flames, which he kept feeding. I did the same, but first I went to the boat for the bag.

"For Button and his family," I said.

The woman and the little boy watched the bag avidly but did not move until Button gave them a sign. With little cries of curiosity and admiration, the woman was examining the jugs, pots and pans, cords, knives. There was also jerked beef and biscuits that the boy and the woman ate at once. Button did not eat. He pointed to the boy:

"Koko-shei," he said.

There was also a pair of gloves. Jemmy inspected everything and then put it all back in the bag. Around the fire, wrapped in a white fog that distorted the sounds in an unnatural way, we seemed to be the only survivors of a world come to an end. It wasn't so; from one or more places we, as well as the ship, were being observed by Button's countrymen.

For a moment I forgot everything. Slowly our old brotherhood found its way back and, like the fire, settled between us. He didn't appear to be surprised by our meeting. When I noted this, he answered that in a dream he had already seen it, my return and our meeting, just as years before in England he had seen his father's death.

"In a dream I saw Jack coming and I told the others."

The confirmation of the dream was something natural. So our meeting was not accidental. The ship had been sighted the very moment its bowsprit appeared at the Beagle Channel's western mouth. Jemmy was glad of my attitude, at my coming to look for him, but it was foreordained that we would meet. I recovered the feeling that Button's logic was the stronger, at least there, and I also accepted the idea that the meeting had been fated.

"White men very bad, Jack."

Searching for words in a tongue to which his mind and his throat were responding a little at a time, Button told me in guttural English what had occurred with his clan.

The previous year had been disastrous. A fierce winter had brought such hunger as had not been suffered on the islands for a long time. One of his wives—or his previous wife, I didn't quite understand—had been raped and murdered by the seal hunters precisely for taking too big a risk in hunting for food. They had dragged her to a rowboat, then to the ship, and the next day they had thrown her overboard. She had fought like a man, but the sealers were five and had firearms. The English had pitched camp on Keppel Island in the Falklands. They transported the Indians, held them a few months, and then returned them to Tierra del Fuego. None of them wanted to go. They did it to maintain an equilibrium, in order not to "make the white men angry." A group of Yámana males had become furious because they wanted them to leave their children at the Mission; in fact, the first of the Englishmen to arrive, called missionaries, had wanted "to hunt" some children by pursuing the women's canoes. There on Keppel the English called them thieves.

Button was impassive as he looked at the fire and recited his litany. Yes, the Yámanas had killed some shipwrecked whites, and whenever they sighted a ship or a boat, they made signs to show that they would kill and eat them in little pieces. It was the only way to scare the rapists and the animal-killers and keep them far away. The seal hunters had wiped out large numbers of pups; none were left, so they weren't able to breed. His people had to look for food far from the coast, in the forests.

To distract him from all these misfortunes, I told him that he had a handsome son. The wholesome food had slipped him into a deep sleep, curled up against the dog who sheltered him near the fire. In the meantime, the woman had gone a couple of times to check the canoe and had come back silently to follow our conversation with curiosity. I asked about the rest of his family. Button was proud; one of his sons, a twelve-year-old, would go through the big ceremony in just a few days. It was a secret place, an island only the Yámanas knew.

"The teachings, Jack," Button said proudly, closing a

circle that had opened into a dizzying tunnel of time back to a moment in the past where something remained that I had not understood in full.

"The teachings," I agreed.

A short time later, I followed his canoe through the mist, gliding noiselessly in a mute white world, as in a dream. The ship was closer than I had imagined. When they tossed me the ladder, he held out his hand.

The silhouettes vaguely outlined by the dying fire and Koko-shei's shining little face were the last things I made out before they vanished without a word, without a murmur, into a cavern of mist and darkness. Button had no interest in meeting the Dutchmen. He hated whites.

I did not imagine, I could not imagine, that the next time I would see Button he would be sitting on the bench of the accused. Only four years later.

# FOLIO SIX

*[Falkland Islands, 1860.*
*In the morning.]*


Distant memories join more recent ones. This is what the story seems to dictate. My last visit to the Islands, only five years ago, remains frozen in time, sharing this quality with my first sojourn with the Captain and the doctor thirty years before.

It was no surprise to confirm that, at this end of the world, the administrative formulas and language I knew in England still endure unchanged. Whenever Great Britain's iron hand needs to appear, like a well-oiled mechanism that is never forgotten or neglected, the two pillars that hold up the Empire's dominion rise into view: the Administration and the Law. As I have said before, Mr. MacDowell or MacDowness, nothing odder than the flimsy wood and stone building called the Palace of Justice, in the farthest corner of the South Atlantic, provided so that the authorities might investigate the murder of men, who, romantically—as Rennie points out in his letter to the *Times*—went out to exercise their own rights over the life and liberty of others about whom they had not the slightest knowledge.

The Yámana affair was not limited to the deplorable massacre. The trial exposed the contradictions the Mission was covering up, especially between its leading members: the Reverend George Pakenham Despard and Captain Parker Snow.


On the long night before the trial in Port Stanley, Smyley himself told me the circumstances in which he had found Button, when he was sent by the Mission to the aid of the *Allen Gardiner*. There had been no news about her in three months. The *Nancy* had looked for her along the channels in

149

the midst of an overwhelming silence. There was something abnormal in that calm, Smyley said, that made the men on deck uneasy. They knew that they were being watched. The smoke columns stayed with them for several miles and then suddenly vanished. When they were opposite Murray Strait, they saw the ship in a small bay. The *Allen Gardiner* was adrift, pitching and rolling, her masts stripped down, without sails or cables.

Smyley was not a man to take fright easily and his crew members were armed. He ordered them to lower a dinghy, and they headed for the beach in the area where the missionaries had built the house. They immediately saw that a disaster had occurred there. They were tying up the boats when, to everyone's shock, a naked white man came screaming out from behind the trees on the beach and, in a kind of mad frenzy, ran for cover among them. It was Alfred Coles. His condition was deplorable, and he could barely get his words out. Smyley sent Coles to the *Nancy* right away and steered for the *Allen Gardiner*.

"There is something spine-chilling about an abandoned ship," Smyley reflected. "Not even one rat had stayed on board."

The men's footsteps sounded hollow on the deserted deck. There was nothing left, the ship had been dismantled down to the last scrap of rope. When they went into the hold, the slap of the water against the hull sounded eerily hollow. For any seaman it was a depressing sight which stirred up superstitious feelings difficult to control.

"All the while," Smyley told me, "we could feel them watching, the lurking eyes of the men in the canoes riveted to our necks, but we could see no one. They were undoubtedly hidden, observing us—with stones ready in their slings—from the bushes on the beach."

Then Smyley did something that made the hair on the necks of his men stand on end. He leaned over the ship's rail and shouted toward the shore at the top of his lungs:

"Jemmy Button!"

The furious wingbeats of several cormorants answered him.

"Jemmy Button!" he called out again with all his strength.

The bay remained calm and silent. As they were preparing to abandon the *Allen Gardiner*, to everyone's astonishment, a hoarse voice froze them all.

"Jemmy Button, here!"

A canoe occupied by five Yámanas appeared from behind the rocky promontory at the entrance to the inlet. Standing in the prow was a man.

"Though I had never seen him," Smyley said, "I knew that savage was Jemmy Button."

Smyley is a typical man of the sea, toughened by hundreds of storms, and his one passion, which he has practiced for decades, is the rescue of the shipwrecked. He is from the United States, renders account to no authority, and England has no jurisdiction over him. He is a practical man unmoved by stories like Jemmy Button's, and he's not interested in Indians. Once he had him on deck, he simply pointed a gun at him while his sailors surrounded him, also armed.

"Button seemed unimpressed by the guns," Smyley said. "If he had been, he would not have brought his canoe as close as he did or come on board, leaving his men below. Only after Button spoke, making it very clear that he wished to come to the Islands to make a declaration, to give an account of the facts, was calm restored. They moved to the *Nancy*, weighed anchor, and turned her prow north.

Smyley went ashore on the Islands with the two witnesses and the terrible news of the murders.


Your letter arrived four months ago today. We are in February. Noon melts the outlines of objects, the horizon dissolves into a motionless reflection. The only thing that continues to exist at this still hour is the cooing of the pigeons which, for some unknown reason, I lie waiting for in bed. Storms gather, burst, and move on, but the downpour hardly relieves the heat. For several weeks now I have been writing at night. In the daytime indolence comes over me. I watch Graciana pouring whole pitchers of rain water on her fine black hair. I am doing nothing, my mind filled with memories and images I haven't managed to write down or known how to describe.

Button's story and the strange destiny which united us pose a question that is still unanswered. One thing I know: the words—good or bad—that I set down on these sheets of paper without being forced to by anyone, have turned to me and, as it were, are staring at me, waiting for an answer I don't have.

For the one who writes it, Mr. MacDowell or Mac-Downess, a story is like a mirror.

There are nights when I feel the unbearable burden of Button's story, the story of his people, as if I or my actions had been responsible for his life and his death. Then his wave of farewell from the *Nancy's* stern returns, a gesture in some way unfathomable, wrapped in the ambiguity which for us whites inevitably enveloped all of Button's actions. Ambiguity that was only dispelled when it became a particular expression in his eyes, a point of confluence in which, or so I believed, we understood each other. But did we truly understand each other or did I only imagine myself sometimes entering Button's ancestral world? What did he in turn see when he looked at me? A comrade, or a pretentious white man who came from the east? These questions open a void in which I don't recognize myself.

At daybreak this morning, I am not ashamed to confess it, I dangled from a thin thread of panic. I clung to Graciana's sleeping body like someone hanging on to the shrouds in a storm.

After a while, unable to sleep, I went out to the patio; the plain was a line drained of colour, without name or end.

The killing of the missionaries had stirred up English public opinion. That rising wave had reached the Islands like a boomerang that returns the importance—magnified by London's opinion—of events that in these inclement latitudes would normally pass without so much scandal. But, in fact, behind Button's trial, there were other interests and decisions involved, which now unfold more clearly before me.

Walking down the only street in Port Stanley, I learned the latest news. People everywhere expressed their own opinions and discussed the case excitedly. Parker Snow, the Mission's captain dismissed by Despard, was not a man to keep his views to himself, and he seemed to be looking for proselytes. His presence had aroused general excitement. He considered himself mortally offended by Despard and the Mission; in London a separate lawsuit for his dismissal had been filed.

In the porticoes lashed by the wind, men in small groups were commenting about what Parker Snow had recently related: the Yámanas were furious at the Mission, which intended to carry off their people. He, Parker Snow himself, had witnessed a spine-chilling scene: he had seen Button, more aggressive than any of the others, with his face painted black and his body covered with white streaks and dots, pacing up and down the beach like a fiend, knowing that the whites were pressing his people into service on their ship. At his signal, the Yámanas on board had thrown off their clothes, leaped into the water, and climbed into their canoes, leaving on deck everything they had brought. A huge bonfire had been lit on the beach, and Button could be made out, a black figure outlined against the flames, with his three hundred men behind him illumined by the fire and some fifty canoes tied up and ready. In his exalted tone, Snow said that he had panicked, weighed anchor, and returned to the Mission to give warning about this, but no one had listened to him.

There were two sides involved: the authorities in Port Stanley and the missionaries on Keppel Island in the western Falklands. Governor Moore had no sympathy for the Mission: English efficiency, a matter of national pride, had been called into question because of that stupid act of carelessness. And Moore had not been in favour of a punitive expedition against the Indians; there were no funds. Nor did the incipient sheep industry nor the colonists want complications with missionaries and Indians. In turn, the Mission headed by the Reverend Despard would not submit to a trial for what had occurred on land and would accept the Governor's authority only in the matter of the loss and abandonment of the ship. As for the settlers, some were sympathetic toward the Yámanas and Jemmy Button. Others, deeply indignant, were all for organizing an expedition and punishing them or, at best, leaving those savages to their own fate.

A huge structure of stone and wood. The Antarctic wind slips down the chimney of the iron stove, producing the peculiar doleful moan those of us who have lived in the south are familiar with, become accustomed to or eventually go mad. This is the Palace of Justice in Port Stanley.

Up in front, a rectangular table with four chairs waited to be occupied by the Island's notables as members of the Trial Court. On the left and right, two other chairs were ready for the single witness and for the accused. Against the wall, a long bench would receive those who, directly or indirectly, had something to say concerning the murder of the missionaries. The place began to fill up early. The long anxious wait of the islanders since learning about the incident had come to a head, and no one wanted to miss the chance of being present at the trial. Button and Coles, the leading actors in the drama, had been Port Stanley's favorite topic for the last few days. Almost nobody knew them, and this created additional suspense.

Long benches had been set up in the courtroom; there were also chairs against the walls as in dance halls, leaving only a narrow aisle for people to circulate. To the right of the panel of judges, a small door led to another room. At the opposite end of the same wall another door opened into a long narrow room where a table had been prepared as a buffet with hot drinks and sandwiches for the recess period.

A friendly atmosphere prevailed, not at all tragic nor equal to the magnitude of the case that was up for trial. In such remote and desolate places, social life is a luxury, and those present could hardly disguise their excitement at finding themselves together for an event that was almost theatrical and reminded them of the civilized world. There were very few women. I spoke with no one and no one spoke to me. I was a stranger like any seaman who had just arrived on a ship. If questioned, I had an answer ready: I was a native of Newport and in Montevideo I had joined the crew of the whaler *Kimberly*. No one came to ask me who I was.

The murmurs went on growing until the side door opened. The people quieted down and took their seats. Many remained standing. My place was good, and I could see and hear without difficulty.

The judges or Investigating Committee were divided into two bodies: on one side Moore, the Governor of the Islands, and the Secretary of the Falkland Islands Company, seated somewhat apart since they had a direct interest in the impending business. On the other, the committee proper, which occupied the table up front: Mr. Fortescue, representative of the Colonial Ministry, and its head, the Duke of Newcastle; Reverend Bull, chaplain of the Islands; the secretary of the Patagonian Mission, and Mr. Logden, a relator or public prosecutor.

The witnesses sat on a long bench against the wall: Reverend Despard, leader of the Patagonian Mission; Mrs.

Despard; Captain Smyley; Mr. Lane, Reverend Despard's lawyer; and Captain Parker Snow, a restless and nervous man. It was ten in the morning according to the wall clock behind the jury, which at that instant started to ring light, musical chimes. They sounded old-fashioned in the silence of the public place.

Mr. Logden moved forward and spoke loudly and clearly.*

MR. LOGDEN:

"This Investigating Committee is assembled in order to elucidate and to render a verdict. First: concerning the abandonment of the British ship *Allen Gardiner* on Navarino Island, in Tierra del Fuego, under sections 432 and 433 of the 1854 Code of the Merchant Marine. Secondly: concerning what occurred on November 6, 1859, in Tierra del Fuego: the massacre of the head catechist, of Captain Fell, and of the entire crew (with one exception) of the missionary ship *Allen Gardiner*, property of the Patagonian Missionary Society. With this purpose, we have had the only survivor and witness of the massacre, Alfred Coles, the cook of the *Allen Gardiner*, come into this court."

The side door opened, and the only direct witness in the case came in, accompanied by a bailiff. They made him take the chair to the right of the judge.

Coles's three months of living among the Yámanas could be seen in his haggard aspect. He was extremely thin, all skin and bones, and his neck had plenty of room to dance

---

* A copy in English of the minutes was affixed to the seven sections of Guevara's account. How they came into his hands is not known. The testimonies of Smyley, Coles and Jemmy Button are textual. We have no record, however, that Rev. Despard, his wife and Parker Snow were present at the trial. Nevertheless, the words attributed to them by Guevara conform almost point for point to letters and documents of the *Public Record Office,* in London (Editor's note).

about inside his shirt collar. Besides being drawn, his face looked horrible; his eyebrows had not yet grown back fully; in keeping with their taste for no facial hair, the Yámanas had shaved them off with sharpened seashells. Instead of a man, Coles looked like a skinny boy who would never be able to come out of his state of shock. His eyes swept the room from end to end without resting on anything.

We hadn't fully taken in Coles's presence when the prosecutor announced:

MR. LOGDEN:
"The prisoner accused of leading the massacre of the missionaries in Wulaia: the Yámana native of Tierra del Fuego, James Button, will now be brought in."

At mention of this name, a wave of tension spread through the room. Everyone tried to see between the heads and shoulders of those in front of them, looking in the direction of the room's side entrance, but the door didn't open. Button must have been awaiting his turn outside and appeared through the main entrance. Those in front noisily turned bodies and chairs around to see him come in. He, like Coles, entered with a bailiff. I watched him advance down the narrow passage now opening between the benches and the knees of those at the front of the room.

Jemmy Button. He had aged in everything but the way he walked and moved. His eyes had sunk deeper in his face, his hands and arms looked like seared tree branches, but his torso was powerful and showed dignity. He was wearing a blue seaman's shirt and shapeless trousers that reached down a little above his ankles. His shaggy hair fell to his shoulders. When he took his place before the silent assembly, he made a face, a kind of slight smile. Perhaps it was because he was once more the centre of the whites' attention or because the unusual reunion of grave and silent men reminded him remotely of the initiation ceremonies in the great wigwam.

Or perhaps it was just a false impression. His enormous flat feet rested on the ground uneasily, looking separate from his body. Accustomed to the sharpness of the rocks, the burning ice, and the cutting edges of seashells, they had a life of their own and were like two small animals on the defensive. Button had now sat down and was digging his heels into the chair's crossbar as if he were looking for a point of support, and he remained like that, apparently calm. I knew how to interpret the almost imperceptible signs that he was prepared and fully alert. He was in a closed place, very uncomfortable for a Yámana.

Two or three times his expressionless eyes swept the room, slipping past my face without showing recognition, but there was a small flicker, a slight change before he sat down; I did not know then whether it was what I really saw or something I imagined. To Button all of us bearded white men might look the same, covered with heavy outer clothing that hid any individual feature of the body. As I found out afterwards, he had recognized me but didn't know if I was there in his favour or as an enemy.

He could not have avoided seeing me. Unaware of it, I had stood up when he came in and remained like that until much later.

There was Omoy-lume, come from Cape Horn of his own free will to testify. I had a disturbing thought, something I felt with a force it would be difficult for you to understand, Mr. MacDowell or MacDowness. This apparently miserable man, a seal hunter who carried fire with him wherever he went as a sign of what he had achieved, of having risen above the animals and above the icy night at the world's end; this man to whom Europeans would find it hard to concede the status of man because for them he lacked the essential attributes for them to call him human—he did not possess their religion or their way of life or their clothes—; this man was definitely the only one in those Islands who had the right to sit on a rock. Men like him had been the natural inhabitants of these lands. He and his people were masters of the ice and the rocks, the only owners of the guanacos and the seals, of the algae and the shellfish on the coast, and they had been for thousands of years.

Neither in the days before the investigation in Port Stanley, nor in my voyages to London, nor on the ships that crossed Cape Horn had I ever heard one word that could reflect an iota of this elemental idea. Its very expression would have scandalized everyone from Governor Moore and the missionaries down to the last person attending the trial. No one was ready even to consider it; in this point they were all of one mind without need for words. And Jemmy, like his people, had begun to suspect it.

What was occurring was out of all proportion. But why had he come? If he had done so, it was because, deep down, the feeling that he was in his own country gave him a slight sense of security. Was that it? Or was it an act of arrogance? Or of daring, of love for his people? Was he going to sacrifice himself for his tribe? Had it occurred to him that by showing up he could be taken prisoner? But above all, how would he return to his islands? I did not know the answer.

Like someone waking up, I once more became conscious of the faces and the angry murmurs of the crowd before the presumably guilty one, the savage. I was the only one standing. Someone tapped me on the shoulder to make me sit again. Button didn't look again in my direction.

The prosecutor pounded on the table to obtain silence. The only thing that worried me was how he would manage to get back, what he could do to make the whites let him return to Wulaia.

MR. LOGDEN:
"The Court requests that Alfred Coles, twenty-three years old, cook of the schooner *Allen Gardiner*, give an account before this Court of the events he witnessed on November 6, 1859."

Coles gave a violent start in his chair. I had the strange feeling that he was exaggerating, perhaps to win the audience's compassion, but even if that were the case, Coles inspired nothing but pity. He was handed a Bible and swore with his hand upon it, as he was prompted to do. He swallowed hard, as if there were something blocking his throat. Time after time, he threw a suspicious glance at Button, who never looked at him once.

ALFRED COLES:

"I was the *Allen Gardiner's* cook when she left Keppel to take the nine natives back to Wulaia, Button's island. They were three men, three women, and three children. We came from Keppel to Stanley. When we left Stanley along the coast, we entered Sparrow Cove, went out by the port of Mare, and from there went to Ship's Port and then to Wulaia. We were in Wulaia two Sundays, and the second Sunday was the day of the massacre, the 6th of November.

"On the morning of the massacre, the whole crew, except me, went ashore, and while I was cooking dinner I noticed that two savages were taking the oars from the boats on the beach. A few minutes later there was a lot of shouting and screaming, and I saw our men come out of the shack running and stumbling down the beach and the natives chasing them with clubs and stones, beating them with the clubs and sticks till they knocked them down on the beach. They were hurling stones in all directions with horrible cries. The wooden shack was about twelve yards from the beach. When they reached the beach they beat them all except the catechist and another man, a Swede, who tried to launch a boat into the water. Then Jemmy Button's son, Billy Button, one of the savages whose belongings had been searched, grabbed a rock and smashed it on the head of catechist Phillips, on one side of his head, where blood spurted and he threw him into the water."

A buzz of horror, especially from the ladies present, spread through the courtroom.

"I saw the murdered captain and his brother side by side on the beach, lying on their blood-smeared faces. I could see them very clearly, and I saw it all, all except old man Hewey murdered on the beach. I lowered a damned boat and jumped in. I rowed as fast as I could, fleeing in the direction of the woods. A canoe had been following me but I got ashore, ran as fast as I could, and went into the woods. The god-damned savages were close behind, but I went in the woods and quickly scrambled up a tree."

Coles's agitation kept him from going on; he was shaking and his shoulders shuddered in a strange way. Amid total silence, Logden placed a hand on his shoulder and looked for a glass of water on the judges' table. Coles gulped it down.

"The natives didn't chase me into the woods. From up in the tree, I saw the savages haul up my boat and take it to the place where the other boats were. After a while, I got down from the tree and went back farther into the woods. I had nothing to eat. Four days later, I went back to the beach and pulled up some limpets from the rocks. After eating limpets and mussels for twelve days, I bumped right into some natives. They didn't do anything to me. They took me with them and gave me some fish and shellfish, but they took away my clothes. They only left me my belt and my earring. They wanted to pull out my beard by the roots, but they couldn't; they shaved my face and my eyebrows with a sharp seashell. I was with these natives for ten days, naked. They took me back to the schooner, travelling with them day after day. There were close to eighteen or twenty of this tribe. When I got back to the schooner, I bumped right into Jemmy Button and his brother Tommy."

Coles was nodding his head as if wanting to confirm it: yes, they were there. He pointed to Button.

"It was them and their group. Everything had been looted, anything that looked like iron pulled up; the lanterns on deck pulled out; hooks and rings from the rigging pulled out; the canvas ripped from the bolt-ropes of the masts. There wasn't a trace of provisions of any kind on board. There was nothing but trash lying around. The fore-and-aft sails had been cut to pieces to take off their steel hooks. They had carried off the wheel and the cabin stairs, pulled right out. From then on, I stayed with the natives, travelling with them all the time, because they go from place to place constantly, till the *Nancy* came to rescue me. I was able to talk to two of the tribe's children who had been at Keppel, and they told me that Jemmy Button and others had gone on board the *Allen Gardiner* the night of the massacre and that Jemmy Button had slept that very night in the Captain's cabin, in the Captain's own bed."

Here Coles pointed out Button again, as if he hadn't made clear who he was talking about. Once more a buzz of shock and indignation ran through the courtroom. Encouraged by the effect he was producing, Coles's shrill voice came out almost in a scream.

"I believe, sir, I believe the reason for the massacre was that Jemmy Button was jealous, envious because he hadn't been given everything he thought he deserved. We hadn't given him presents! He doesn't like white people…! I am sure he was the instigator, the head of the whole massacre!"

He was trembling from head to foot. They made him sit down for a moment, but he was immediately back on his feet, overcome by his own nerves.

"What happened to the carcasses…"

MR. LOGDEN:
"What do you mean by carcasses?"

ALFRED COLES:
"The dead bodies. I don't know what happened to those bodies. I don't know if they were eaten, or burned or tossed into the water. One of the Indian boys also told me they had seen Jemmy fighting. I couldn't tell him from the rest, all of them with painted faces. I can't tell about him but I can tell about Billy Button: it was the son who killed the catechist. I think there must have been about three hundred altogether, including women and children, before the killers came, and they were scream-ing the whole time we were there. When I went back to the place, only Jemmy Button, his family, and a few others were there. He told me there was still one man alive. I didn't believe him at all. I had seen them murder everybody except old Hewey, and the boys had told me that they had killed him in the shack. I went to the shack many times. There was no floor, there was no trace of anything. I went on board and made my declaration to Captain Smyley."

MR. LOGDEN:
"Did they search the bags of the natives?"

ALFRED COLES:

"Yes. They searched them the day after they got into Wulaia because a lot of things had been lost. The captain insisted on looking for them."

MR. LANE:

"I object to that question!"

Reverend Despard's attorney had jumped to his feet abruptly.

"This part of the investigation cannot be extended to include the reason for the loss of human life on the coasts of Tierra del Fuego. Furthermore, proving the jurisdiction depends on the words 'in another part,' and so there is no authority assigned to the Ministry of Commerce in the Falkland Islands to conduct this investigation."

The secretary assented.

MR. LOGDEN:

"Was the loss of human lives on the coast the reason for abandoning ship?"

ALFRED COLES:

"Yes."

MR. LANE:

"An investigation of the reasons for the loss of human life is not within the jurisdiction of the Act of Parliament, which limits the investigation to the reason for abandoning ship."

The judges held a consultation. Reverend Despard followed the deliberations with his eyes fixed on them. Mr. Fortescue, spokesman for the Colonial Ministry, said:

MR. FORTESCUE:

"The Court is of the opinion that there exists absolute authority to investigate any situation which occurs on board a vessel, as in this case, as well as any situation involving the loss of human life. Therefore, having underscored the fact that the abandonment of the ship was due to the loss of human life on the coast, we can now proceed with the second part of the investigation: the causes of the massacre. Proceed."

MR. LOGDEN:

"Did they search the natives upon arrival in Wulaia?"

ALFRED COLES:

"They searched the bags of the natives who were on board because some things had disappeared, and among their clothes they found a harpoon, a silk handkerchief, and a steel knife. This wasn't to the liking of the savages, who had refused to be searched. They were very angry. One of them, a husky fellow named Swyamuggins, seized the captain by the throat and held him up in the air over the gangplank. The captain had to strike him a blow to defend himself. Afterwards they jumped into their canoes and went off to the coast. Billy Button was one of them."

MR. LOGDEN:

"During the fifteen days that they were on Navarino Island, before the massacre, were the captain and his men armed?"

ALFRED COLES:

"They were armed with axes to cut firewood."

MR. LOGDEN:

"The witness may sit down."

Coles appeared calmer. He returned to his chair.

MR. LOGDEN:
"The Court now calls the superintendent of the Patagonian Mission, the Reverend Despard, to testify."

Despard, a thin man, dressed in black, stood up and advanced
a few steps. Logden held the Bible in his hand.

REVEREND DESPARD:
"I refuse to take the oath."

THE COURT:
"You are advised that you must do it."

After pondering for a few moments, Despard took the oath
with his hand on the Bible.

MR. LOGDEN:
"Reverend Despard, can you give us some evidence as to
what made the natives abandon the ship?"

REVEREND DESPARD:
"I cannot."

MR. LOGDEN:
"Do you know of any threat or threatening words used
by the natives on Keppel before embarking?"

REVEREND DESPARD:
"I refuse to answer."

MR. LOGDEN:
"Did you hear any threat?"

REVEREND DESPARD:

"I have no precise memory of this."

MR. LOGDEN:

"Did the natives on Keppel attempt at any time to pro-
voke an act of rebellion or did they ever threaten the
colonists or missionaries?"

REVEREND DESPARD:

"No."

MR. LOGDEN:

"Did you search the bags of the natives on Keppel?"

REVEREND DESPARD:

"I refuse to answer."

It was clear that the head of the Patagonian Mission had much
to lose. At the other end of the witness bench, the first captain
of the *Allen Gardiner*, Parker Snow, dismissed by Despard
for insubordination, was fidgeting nervously. His excuse had
been expressed in violent words against the Mission in the
*Times* which I possess and have already mentioned. It was
obvious that he was seeking public revenge and, with that in
mind, he had been up and down the streets of Stanley on the
previous day. He would not look at Despard when the latter
spoke.

Button remained motionless all the while. One might
almost say that they had forgotten that he was there. I
supposed that the heat in the room must be suffocating him.
The part referring to the abandonment of the ship had ended.
Despard made signs that he wanted to be allowed to speak
later. Mrs. Despard, on the bench beside her husband, seemed
to suffer a fainting spell. Another woman came over and
fanned her with a handkerchief, and the bailiff next to Coles
fetched her a glass of water. This scene was taking place

behind the back of the prosecutor who, unaware of what was occurring there, had started to speak a few minutes before. Mrs. Despard appeared to recover. Coles, his shoulders and back bent, his hands between his knees, was staring absently at the back of the room.

MR. LOGDEN:

"...you may imagine, then, gentlemen of the tribunal, the shudder of horror that shook London the morning that the ordinary citizen was able to read that in Cape Horn there had taken place the worst treachery anyone could imagine. There, the Anglican missionary members of the altruistic enterprise of Allen Gardiner—who a decade before, after his vessel was shipwrecked, had starved to death in a cave surrounded by Indians—had arrived in a schooner named precisely *The Allen Gardiner* and, with missionary zeal, under the distant neutral eyes of the Yámanas watching from their canoes or from the beaches close by, had built a wooden structure, a shelter to house their religious services. There on Sunday, November 6, 1859, while Coles the cook remained on board (the only one excused from religious services) to await their return with a festive lunch and—as a consequence of this very circumstance—the only living witness of what took place on that morning which later on was inevitably described in London as the morning on which the Christian faith overcame the untamed savage. There the treacherous Indians waited for the missionaries to start singing their hymns inside the shelter before attacking and murdering them, as we have already heard, without an atom of mercy. If this was known, if this came to be known, it was because a horrified Coles went up from the kitchen to the deck and there, clinging to the ship's rail, witnessed the most atrocious massacre human eyes could witness without going mad."

The prosecutor paused, went to the table, and poured himself a glass of water; he drank it.

"But, gentlemen, this entire horrible story contains something worse, something even more sinister than what I have just been telling you, because the one who led this massacre, the one who committed this crime not only against the Patagonian Mission but against England, was someone whom England had taken in and educated, someone on whom England had pinned its hopes for civilizing and rescuing from barbaric darkness, from a jabbering naked state and from the inclement weather, to raise him to the level of the English language, to the use of decent clothing, and to civilization. It was someone who had been given the privilege of a royal audience and on whom the eyes of our sovereign had rested with hope and pity."

At that moment I could not help but remember, nor can I now, Mr. MacDowell or MacDowness, William IV's justified reputation as a drunkard and a libertine.

"This man taken to London and returned to Cape Horn with an education was the hope for a bond of friendship, and he repaid the kingdom with the murder of innocent missionaries."

As had occurred in the case of Coles, we all looked at Button, sitting in his chair, to the left of the dais. Not even one gesture divulged whether or not he had understood what the prosecutor had said.

MR. FORTESCUE:
"The Court now calls on the superintendent of the Patagonian Mission, the Reverend Despard, to testify."

Despard left his place on the bench next to his wife and advanced a few steps.

REVEREND DESPARD:

"I am only taking the stand to show good will. This case will continue before a court in London, where I shall present all the points in my defense. Having made this statement, allow me now to retreat back to the past. This man, this native called Jemmy Button, was purchased for five buttons twenty-five years ago by Captain Robert FitzRoy and taken to England. He was treated with extreme kindness and taken back to his home two years later. The Mission contacted him when we settled on Keppel, and we placed our trust in him. Last year, under no pressure of any kind, this man brought his wife and three children to the Mission, and they lived here with me. He was treated with hospitality and indulgence, his clothing was washed for him, bread was baked for him every week, he moved among us with absolute freedom, and he had to do no work except keep his house and utensils clean..."

PARKER SNOW:

"I object! I object to everything he is saying!"

He had jumped to his feet and, with no one able to stop him, he spoke in a rush of excited words.

PARKER SNOW:

"As I have already said time and again, I am asking for justice and I call the attention of your Excellency's Government to the actions of the Patagonian Mission! I was forced to leave my position for openly expressing my opinion and refusing to collaborate with the Mission's staff, who were deceiving the natives. The Mission's plan of operation was to take the natives by force to Keppel

Island, make them work without pay, since they would have no way to escape from there... I was discharged without a second thought! I have received absolutely no justice despite my repeated appeals to the authorities. The Patagonian Missionary Society together with Her Majesty's government are responsible before our country for the actions permitted their officials and for the killing of our companions in Wulaia, but why should I be surprised...?"

MR. LOGDEN:
"Please return to your place until you are called."

PARKER SNOW:
"Why should I be surprised? I am only one more among thousands, as jurisprudence testifies: whoever opposes the influence of wealth or power cannot hope to procure justice!"

MR. LOGDEN:
"Enough! Witness Parker Snow will testify when this Court calls him. Please sit down."

A growing murmur ran through the courtroom. With great difficulty, an official was able to make the former captain of the *Allen Gardiner* return to his place. Indignant, Mrs. Despard was shaking her head, and Reverend Despard was speaking to his attorney, Mr. Lane. It took a few minutes to restore order. Logden asked Reverend Despard to continue. The man seemed on the verge of breaking down. He recovered immediately and continued.

REVEREND DESPARD:
"Button and his wife were brought to the Islands with good will a year ago. He seemed truly happy to show his English friends his sons, especially the oldest, approxi-

mately eight years old, to whom we tried to impart some knowledge of God, Our Lord. But the boy needed more time before he could understand, for he had only learned a few words of English. They spent the winter and spring with us in our missionary station and won our good will, something to which Mrs. Despard can well attest…"

No one objected to his letting his wife participate without the Court's having called her and without being sworn in. The reverend seemed to be crushed and yielded the floor to his wife, who did not hesitate to continue. Her hands were clasped, pressing a handkerchief to her chest.

MRS. DESPARD:
"I must say that when they left us to go back to Tierra del Fuego we missed them very much. They never did anything to offend or displease us: Jemmy was extremely obliging. I had never seen Jemmy more grateful. He was always clean."

Mrs. Despard cast an involuntary glance to where Button sat but he remained impassive, his eyes half-closed. Mrs. Despard was speaking unaffectedly, as if she were referring to a house dog.

"Jemmy remembered his English very well, and he understood us better than we could understand them. He knew, he knew that there is a God Creator of all things and he knew of our Holy Saviour. And yet… I said to him, 'Jemmy, will you come back with us?' And he said that he could not promise it. 'Maybe,' he said, 'I can't promise now.' The Fuegians are very lazy; they never went to look for firewood. One day I said to him, 'James, God loves good men; good men are not lazy. God doesn't love good-for-nothings,' and he agreed, letting me know that he had understood. He was soon working hard at the

Mission. And you should have heard his family. 'If you wish,' 'thank you,' 'good day'—one heard this all the time, in English, of course. They gave thanks for their meals and said their nightly prayers. I couldn't help being pleased at seeing how the little dark-skinned one, the small boy, progressed under the instruction of my children... All that work! All that work, and now this disgrace...! At last they were decent with their own clothes, decently dressed, not naked, with clean clothing, not with the nauseating smell of grease and smoke. It must be said: clothed and with the knowledge of God. That is how Jemmy Button went away from the Mission on Keppel Island."

PARKER SNOW:

"With all respect to the lady and the Court, I must point something out. At the Mission they fancied that they had made the Fuegians happy with clothes, prayer, and work. However, Button..."

MR. LOGDEN:

"Wait for your turn to speak..."

PARKER SNOW:

"Button was at Keppel against his will! Upon our return in the ship, he begged us near Wulaia to put him ashore with his family before arriving... He wished to continue by land. No doubt fearing that the ship would turn around..."

MR. LOGDEN:

"This Court warns you, Mr. Snow, that if you do not respect your turn, you shall not be able to speak later on."

ATTORNEY LANE:

"The Reverend Despard refuses to participate directly in this trial. He asks me to read his allegation addressed to the Duke of Newcastle."

From Lane's reading it was clear that Despard was not openly accusing Button but considered that though he had not taken part in the massacre, neither had he done anything to prevent it. He spoke about the life at the Mission. Lane went on reading the document written by Despard.

ATTORNEY LANE:

"Once they attempted to break into our larder in search of molasses. I let them see how displeased I was by depriving them of the plum pie they ate every Sunday, and they never again repeated this attempt. They had stolen some small articles and tools that belonged to the workers, and as they knew that stealing was bad, I decided that they must not continue in that sin. When they were boarding ship on the way to Wulaia, I gave orders that their bags and boxes be searched in everyone's presence, and the missing articles were found among their belongings and recovered. When they were being searched they appeared nervous, but that is how the guilty thief acts. We ended up as very good friends.

"It should be observed that the natives knew full well where they were going, why and for how long, and that there was no attempt to abduct them, and they received no treatment which could have led them to commit a massacre.

"It is clear which natives committed the massacre; Governor Moore need not dig very deep to find them. Avarice, avarice for the possession of a ship they knew was full of an immense treasure of clothing, foodstuffs and tools. Three hundred men ignorant of God, of the Final Judgment, of morality, with nothing to stop them except fear, those unchristened savages coveting the riches of an enormous ship. They had a convenient opportunity when the missionaries went ashore.

"Your Lordship, considering these circumstances, we have the right to believe that our last guests were the instigators of the massacre and to ascribe it to their hurt feelings.

"I refuse to be interrogated by this court because it has been instituted by those who will distort my answers in order to justify their own ideas. Nevertheless, before a just court and a proper judge I am prepared to explain that I have conducted myself before the natives as someone who loves them and desires to bring them close to Jesus Christ, Our Saviour, for without Him neither they, nor I, nor you, your Lordship, can attain eternal life.

"The cause of this disaster was simple avarice and not maltreatment. The repetition of a similar catastrophe can be prevented if the captain of the ship takes the necessary precautions and measures to prevent it.

"Your Excellency will not, I am sure, recommend that a British colony be deprived of the great honour of becoming a centre of the greatest blessings that may be conferred in spite of and above the most despicable persons."

It was clear that the sole purpose of Despard's forced attendance at this trial was to make his position irreproachable and at the same time discredit the court of the Islands. Moore was talking to Reverend Bull. The conversation became general, with everyone giving his opinion, almost shouting in the midst of growing disorder.

The close atmosphere and the crush of people oppressed me. It once more occurred to me that Button must have found the heat unbearable. I got up as discreetly as I could and went out. The sharp sea air hit my face. I walked a few steps toward the beach, filling the bowl of my pipe with tobacco and mulling over everything I had heard.

Despard seemed to be thoroughly crushed. It was obvious that his world had collapsed on top of him. His forced attendance at the trial had drained most of his strength. I could imagine the kind of mystic thoughts that accosted him. God's fatherly hand had rested on his shoulder and had led him with infinite love toward these abject creatures. Nevertheless, an atrocious emptiness had settled within him since all this had taken place. He was guilty of having sent a whole crew to the slaughter. His blind trust in the Mission, the support he had won for it in England... Letters, words of encouragement for him and his undertaking had arrived from all over; they had been heaped with blessings and these blessings had surrounded them, had protected them on their way to this land so much in need of God. And he had been the one chosen to bring His Word. He had placed his trust in Jemmy Button who was now under suspicion of murder. All the stress, all the sorrows of life in these horrid and hostile places had been in vain. Mrs. Despard could never shed enough tears to weep for the years of her youth withered by this fierce wind that even seemed to do away with Divine mercy. Doubtless, Despard must be feeling something like this, I thought as I emptied my pipe. It was all over, and he would hand in his resignation. Perhaps this last part was merely wishful thinking on my part.

When I went in again, the prosecutor was speaking.

MR. LOGDEN:
"The Court will take an hour's recess."

# FOLIO SEVEN

*[Falkland Islands 1860.*
*In the afternoon.]*


I have used the recess to drink some maté. I awakened
Graciana and I have asked her to feed me. I didn't sleep all
night, I couldn't. It's almost daylight here, Mr. MacDowell
or MacDowness, while there the long afternoon of the Islands
is beginning; the heat is oppressive here, while there a cold
wind blows; here it's now, there it's five years ago; here I'm
sipping maté, something that, if I had to, I wouldn't know
how to explain. I'll try: it's a brew, the equivalent of your
five o'clock tea. It's odd, this story is not meant for you, but
I have become accustomed to your name, or perhaps I should
say your names and it's as if I know you now.

In the Islands, during the recess, we didn't drink tea or
maté but hot punch. Here, the plain to the east is beginning
to turn a lilac colour. Through the courtroom's window, the
sea was starting to turn dark.


The rumor reached me that Despard was leaving the trial and
would await the result somewhere else before sailing to
Keppel. The rumor was circulating in the crowded room next
to the courtroom, where one could have something to eat
and drink. With much difficulty I had managed to work my
way to the table and get back to one of the windows where,
with my back to the wall, I held a glass of hot punch and a
small portion of bread with roast lamb.

Except for Smyley, I didn't know anyone, and since
Smyley wasn't in there, I was all alone, listening to what was
being said.

Parker Snow's outrage provoked supporters as well as
opponents. Some said he had foreseen what would occur,
that he was a man with experience and that Despard was a

despot. Others backed the missionaries and their work. The wave of conversation swelled and the voices drowned out one another. The rivalry between Despard and Governor Moore was also discussed, especially Despard's refusal to accept the Court's authority.

I turned to the window and immersed myself in the desolate landscape of the Islands. In the good natural harbor several ships were rocking at anchor and among them I recognized the *Nancy*, the *Davidson,* and the *Kimberly*, the whaler in which I had come.

The recess ended and we slowly made our way back to our places. The clock now showed three in the afternoon. Reverend Despard and his wife were no longer on the witness bench.

Parker Snow was waiting for his turn standing up, apparently unable to sit because of his very visible excitement. Looking tired, Governor Moore leaned across the table and said something in Logden's ear. Everything was now ready.

MR. LOGDEN:
"The Court calls Captain Parker Snow to the stand."

PARKER SNOW:
"Gentlemen of the Court, on several occasions during the past three years I have written to Her Majesty's government with regard to my denunciation of the authorities of the Falkland Islands and their predisposition in favour of the Patagonian Missionary Society and of the injustice to me and of my ruin. At first I believed I would receive satisfaction. I was näive enough to believe that the justice of my cause would be enough. Now I know that if a man is poor and has no friends and stands up against religious groups or those connected to the government, he cannot expect the truth to be made clear and to obtain satisfaction. Now, having learned this

lesson, I turn to his Lordship the Duke and his representative, Mr. Fortescue, no longer as a petitioner but as
a person who has the rights of kings."

At this point Snow gave Fortescue a meaningful look. His
words provoked uneasiness in the court and in the audience
as well. Button leaned against the back of his chair and, like
Coles, seemed to be absent from the room.

"The tremendous massacre of a ship has taken place. I
saw it coming and alerted the authorities; I warned our
country's government and pleaded that it step in and
prevent those men who, under the name of "missionaries," would uproot the natives without considering the
consequences, going ahead with the Mission's plan and
thus gaining access to public money…"

MR. LANE:
"I ask the Court not to consider what this gentleman has
just insinuated…"

MR. LOGDEN:
"Later on you may object in the name of Reverend
Despard. Let the witness continue."

PARKER SNOW:
"I offered to prove that the Mission's whole plan was not
only deceitful but also dangerous for all concerned. But
of course no one listened to my voice. And now you can
see the results! An entire crew sacrificed! When I occupied the position of ship's captain, I opposed the ways of
the missionary superintendent Despard, who has now
preferred to absent himself instead of listening to my
truths."

He spoke in a slow-paced, persuasive tone, like someone explaining something he had explained a thousand times. He threw the audience an ironic glance. He possessed a certain histrionic ability and was making use of it.

"I was not going to be among those who would bring people forcibly to Keppel Island for the sole purpose of starting a colony, or rather, to show that colonization would succeed. The plan of operation was to bring the natives by hook or by crook and make them work, since once they were taken there, they could not escape. It confirmed my views when I heard the opinion of the former Governor of the Islands, Mr. Rennie, who was not slow to point out that such an action would constitute a kidnapping."

The Court signalled to Logden, who came over. Then he eyed the witness.

MR. LOGDEN:
"Is this opinion of ex-Governor Rennie's to be found anywhere?"

I had the impression that Parker had just been waiting to be asked this question.

PARKER SNOW:
"Yes, sir. It is. It's in his letter to the London *Times* of December 10th, 1859, a newspaper I have brought along and have in my possession."

MR. LOGDEN:
"Go on."

PARKER SNOW:
"The Society practiced delays, slander, abuses; they held

meetings throughout the kingdom to raise funds, and they squandered the money that should have been used for the Mission's expenses. But it was their verdict. I had disobeyed orders, and though I was not crazy but deeply aware of the cruelty and perversity of this business of deporting natives, and though I had been in charge of the *Allen Gardiner* for two years, and though the Society had expressed its thanks to me, the Law said I was only a machine and that, having disobeyed the orders of the head missionary, I must suffer. And I have suffered, together with my wife. The reason that I now address Your Excellency, through your representative, is to request that you order an investigation and put a stop to these senseless acts consented to by the government's officials. Five years ago, when I was in charge, the authorities told me that bringing natives against their will could be considered kidnapping, as I have just said, or even homicide if some disaster occurred. Now that a whole crew has been massacred by the natives, without any doubt to take revenge against the missionaries who carried off their children and their relatives by force, I realize that those charges would be brought against me alone—because I am poor and have no friends—and not against Captain Sulivan, who replaced me, nor against the Mission, with which he was in full accord. I ask: is it because they have the means and influence to do almost anything they please? Sir, is there no one who can see this? Will no government question and investigate how the natives had been taken from Tierra del Fuego to Keppel? At first, I had orders to bring two Fuegians so that the Mission might let people know, through their propaganda in England, that 'the natives were living at the Mission station.' I realized at once that there was a great risk involved. Furthermore, on that first passage my instructions were to find Jemmy Button and take him to Keppel. They all believed this native educated in

England would provide their safe-conduct, he would be a priceless advantage in the hard task of establishing the first contacts with the natives. Everything seemed simple from there on. Well, all right, the man I ran into was this one."

Parker Snow pointed directly at Button.

"He was naked and his aspect was in every way like that of his people. And this poor creature had been the favourite idol of London, he had been introduced to royalty, and finally, he had been sent back to Tierra del Fuego as a fairly well-educated man! Really, gentlemen, I could not believe my eyes, and my astonishment grew when he greeted me with broken words in my own language. But I had to act immediately because, in his impatience, the catechist wished to trap some of the children in the canoes. Fortunately I was able to stop him. The Fuegians were never able to understand the Mission's motives; all they understand is that the white men snatched away their little ones and wished to take them, they don't know why, to a place very far away from their islands. I realized that vengeance might follow. The natives did not want to be treated this way. And I repeat: it's nothing but slavery that is being practiced when a Fuegian is taken to Keppel, where they make him work, use the language of the Missionary Society, and do all they can to keep him from escaping. Well now, because I saw all this I was dismissed, abandoned along with my wife in Stanley, without money, condemned to go up and down the hills to procure something by selling our household goods— since the Mission paid me off with a used rug and some pork—and thus be able to purchase our passage back to England. They have not listened to me. They have not listened to me at all."

He paused a moment to catch his breath. He asked for a glass of water, and it was brought to him.

> "When the new governor, Mr. Moore, the gentleman representing the Duke, arrived, he advised me in the beginning not to do what Despard asked of me. However, later on he and his officials collaborated with the Mission to provoke my dismissal. They rejected any investigation that might have prevented this massacre. The aim of the Colonial Ministry is to do justice, and it must attend to the most insignificant as well as the most powerful person. And yet this does not occur. The Mission has official support and I am nobody. There's Captain Sulivan, my successor! He is the head of a government department! So then, does the Mission have official support or not? Isn't Sulivan in fact a principal active member of this Missionary Society? And hasn't he tried to make the colony function with the work of the natives? I have it all written down and proved!"

Mr. Fortescue made a discreet sign to Mr. Logden to draw near. Parker Snow did not see this but we did. There was quick deliberation. The people in the courtroom fidgeted uncomfortably in their seats. Parker Snow was a man who upset many people in Port Stanley, and very few were interested in having him display his eloquence with details.

MR. LOGDEN:
> "The Court requests that the witness finish explaining his most significant points in order to leave time for other pertinent testimonies."

At this point Parker Snow did something unexpected: he laughed. He shook his head as if to indicate that this and nothing else could be expected of the Court. He slowly ran his eyes over the crowd.

PARKER SNOW:

"I understand, your Lordship, don't think that I don't understand. And I'll come to the point. It doesn't escape me that Parker Snow will not be heard here, either. Nevertheless, these are my main points."

What he did then is still very vivid in my mind. With the index finger of his right hand he was gradually pulling back, one at a time, the fingers of his left hand.

"First: Parker Snow was forced to leave his post for openly expressing his opinion and refusing to form a new cattle colony on Keppel, where the natives were tricked, brought there against their will, and made to work without being able to escape. Second: Captain Parker Snow was in favour of an investigation that would not only demonstrate the error being committed in relation to the natives but would also prove that the plan of the missionary Despard and his companions was a commercial venture under the name of "Mission." But they refused to listen to the evidence! Third: While all this was happening, the colonial authorities were receiving favours from missionary Despard and his group, and when Captain Snow's ship was seized and detained by a magistrate's order here in Stanley, that same magistrate was drinking and smoking with Despard's attorney, in the attorney's house and observing events from there. Fourth: When compensation for Captain Snow was requested, the magistrate refused and Parker Snow was advised that he would be able to do nothing, since the said magistrate had a friend in the Colonial Ministry who would forestall any investigation. And last of all, if I am speaking for the benefit of anyone, there were officials in the government who for their own advantage backed this Mission in its wrongful acts! Despard and the Commission boasted of their backing by influential persons, one of whom was Captain Sulivan, head of the Marine Department of the Ministry of Commerce, who could use all his weight and influence to hurt Parker Snow. And it was he, Sulivan himself, who made the plans and gave the instructions for the formation of the cattle colony in the Western Falklands, in other words on Keppel, since he was a partner in a cattle company in these Islands and was anxious to sell 134 head to the Missionary Society, on condition that he and his partners divide the profits!"

A murmur of protest broke out in the courtroom. Alfred Coles, who was dozing peacefully with his head fallen to one side, jumped up in his seat. Moore and Fortescue looked at each other. The prosecutor pounded on the table, asking for order. Snow continued, almost shouting.

"I can prove everything I am declaring. Having said all this, Mr. Fortescue, representing his Lordship the Duke of Newcastle, this hateful Patagonian Missionary Society — abominated by God and men, deplored by the rightful impartial opinion of the people—, though it is protected by the government, will be an example of shame and dishonour wherever it goes! And I am not doing this just for myself! The poor who suffer and the thousands of tormented souls on earth stir feelings in my heart which, even if it takes me my whole life, I shall express and spread by word of mouth in every corner of the planet where I may be. Many of those who know me well know how much I love the old institutions and how much respect I have for authority but, your Lordship, people are not just machines to be used like cheap clay without being able to open their mouths when they are wronged. My dear wife and I have been deeply wronged by the Patagonian Missionary Society supported and defended

by the officials of the Crown in these Islands, and it is
because of their actions that I call for justice!"


A heavy silence no one dared to interrupt fell over the courtroom. Visibly exhausted by the nervous strain, Parker Snow
had sat down in his place once more. It was nearly four
o'clock in the afternoon.

The Court summoned Logden and they held council for
a moment. Then the prosecutor addressed the public.

MR. LOGDEN:
"The Court will take a fifteen minute recess before considering James Button's defense. We ask the public to
remain in their places."


Must I make it clear, Mr. MacDowell or MacDowness, that
like all those present in the room, I was impressed by Captain
Parker Snow's declarations? And yet, behind that tangled
skein of interests there was one interest missing. And it was
that of the Yámanas. The reasons put forward so far were not
the cause of the massacre. A long, a very long string of abuses
of every kind led the masters of Cape Horn, the inhabitants
of Tierra del Fuego, to this slaughter. For Button's clan, all
the men who came from the east were the same and their
reasons no longer mattered. They were all abusers, and yet
no one had ever asked them who they were nor had they ever
given any thought to their rights. It amazed me that this
should never even have entered the minds of those pigheaded
people. There was no restitution or justice for Button. The
Fuegians had learned to detest the white man and there was
no going back from there. They just wanted them to leave
their land for good.


A few minutes later the side door opened, and the Court made
their entrance once more.

MR. LOGDEN:

"The Court asks the Fuegian prisoner James Button to take the stand."

The bailiff next to Jemmy tapped him on the shoulder to let him know he was to speak. Button got to his feet. His eyes remained calm in their sunken sockets. He had appeared in court and had sworn on a Bible. Once more, perhaps for the last time, he was a man attentive to our strange rites and ceremonies, and there he stood now, without a trace of fear, looking straight ahead but aware of everything.

JAMES BUTTON:

"I stayed at Keppel Island four moons, with wife and children. Did not like to stop; don't want to; don't like it. Despard say, 'Go back, Jemmy; you're old; your children stop.' Would like children to stop at Wulaia; want to go back, all like to go back Wulaia."

Button's guttural English was gradually awakening from a lethargy of almost thirty years. His ideas searched that language for their sound, at first without finding it, but little by little he succeeded in joining word after word and phrase after phrase. Hearing him, I felt what surely no one in the courtroom could help but feel: whatever his appearance might be, this was no ordinary man. The prosecutor Logden himself seemed to be impressed. After a pause, he asked, without hostility, if the Reverend Despard had ever asked him to go to Keppel.

"Mr. Despard said, 'Go two times to Keppel, two times a year Wulaia; no work at Keppel. Cask of water a big tub at Keppel; spear fish at Keppel, no catch seal, catch fish, big fish.' Our country boy very angry boy when Despard look into bags. Oen's countrymen killed Captain Fell; all same Patagonians bow and arrow men. My country is a small channel, others from big waters; my country near Wulaia, theirs near Patagonia. Oen's country boys say we no kill you; you go away, we kill them. Captain Fell was killed with stones by Oen's country. I see Captain Fell killed; carpenter; another man saw one killed; I no see R. Phillips killed. I put four in the ground. I no see the others. I will show Captain Smyley. I no see no one live; I think one get away in the field, run away. I bury Captain Fell, and the carpenter, and two other Swedes. I no sleep in schooner, run about all around island, no see white man. We look for body Captain Fell my brother say, all by ground near house, my brother dig. Every tribe speaks differently, woman at Wulaia is 'keepa'; my tribe has fifteen canoes, plenty canoes other side over water, plenty. York people no speak Wulaia, Oen's country no speak. York's country two ships broke long time ago. York man eat man, scracht country. My brother perhaps go back to Keppel. I had plenty of it, no want go back; been away three times; country men perhaps go back. My country boy no want to go back to Keppel."

It was the last imposition of the whites on Button and it was, surely, his last concession to the English. This is what he had to say, and he had said it in English.

I have used the language he used. I have used, this time only, Mallory's tongue. It's one of this story's great ironies. But in the event that one of my countrymen should some day read this account, I'm going to translate what Button said. And I am going to explain what, in my judgment, he wished to say:

"I was at Keppel Island for four moons, with wife and children. I didn't like staying there; I didn't want to, didn't like it. Despard said: 'Go back, Jemmy, you are old, but let your children stay.' I wanted the children to stay in Wulaia; I wanted to go back; we all wanted to go back."

(Button made it very clear that his passage to Keppel had been one way to appease the whites who had landed with news about a Mission. It had been a voyage and a stay for reconnaissance.)

Question: "Did Mr. Despard ask you to go to Keppel?"

Answer: "Despard said, 'Go to Keppel two times; two times (equal to) one year in Wulaia; I don't work in Keppel, a cask of fresh water is a large barrel in Keppel; you will fish with a harpoon in Keppel, you will not catch seals but fish, a big fish.' I didn't see them (the sailors) search the bags; one of our boys very angry when Despard looked in the bags. The Oens killed Captain Fell. Just like the Patagonians, men with bow and arrow. My country is in a small channel, the others come from the big waters. My country is Wulaia, theirs is close to Patagonia."

(In other words, Button admitted his people's anger because of the search, for it would have been silly to deny it, but he implicated Reverend Despard and at the same time he blamed his ancestral enemies, the Oens, whom he described as fierce.)

"The Oens said to me: we will not kill you people, go away, we'll kill them. I put four in the ground. I didn't see the others. I buried Captain Fell, the carpenter, and two other Swedes. I didn't sleep in the schooner, I wandered about inland; I didn't sleep any more, I wandered. I was on all the islands around there, I saw no white men. 'We're looking for Captain Fell's body,' my brother said. My brother dug in all the ground near the house."

(In the end this was Button's alibi so he could return to Wulaia. He had buried the bodies. He knew the whites would want to recover them and bury them according to their rites. He knew where they were, and therefore they must take him back to show them the place.)

"Each tribe speaks different, in Wulaia woman is 'kipa.' My tribe has fifteen canoes, there are many canoes on the other side of the water, many. York's people don't speak

Wulaia. In the country of the Oens they don't speak, they don't speak. A long time ago in York's country two ships were wrecked; York's people eat human flesh, dangerous country."

(Button was giving the whites clues to let them know that they were not all the same people in Tierra del Fuego, and that its inhabitants spoke different languages. What's more, it was a region inhabited by cannibals, something that Jemmy knew very well terrified the Europeans. Therefore a dangerous place. Better not go there.)

"Maybe my brother will go back to Keppel. I've had enough, I don't want to go back; I was away from my country three times. Maybe my countrymen will go back, but my countrymen don't want to go back to Keppel."

(With this ambiguous promise Button protected his brother and made it clear that they wanted nothing to do with the Mission. The words *three times* also took in the voyage to England.)


In spite of everything, I was disappointed. Absurdly, I had imagined an allegation by Button that it would have been impossible for him to make. He was not interested in the whites, he had nothing to say to them and had no desire to reveal anything to them. He was acting the part of the well-meaning "ill-starred native." He had really come to find out what their intentions were after the massacre, to find out if there would be a punitive expedition. He only had to bring a valid excuse to have them take him back. And he had already stated it.

Everything had now been said. Logden announced that the Court would retire to deliberate.

I kept my eyes on Button and questions shot through my mind like sharp claws? What was all this farce? Or didn't these respectable men and women understand the limits to which they had driven the Yámanas? Didn't they know that the sealers and whalers had clubbed to death entire droves of seals and sea lions, foxes and guanacos, carrying off the food, killing just to kill? Didn't they know that they had raped their women and young girls, generally the small girls because the women fought as fiercely as the men, and in order to subdue them they often had to beat them to death, while the little girls were like the seals, much easier to trap, much more suited to amuse those unhinged men? Didn't they know that these monstrous unions resulted in bastard children brought up by the Yámanas? Didn't they know that other men of more inoffensive aspect, known as scientists, smeared a white paste on their faces to make masks and exhibited them in distant countries, and that this process had sometimes caused death by asphyxia, or about humiliating tests on the genitals and breasts of women or on the boys who innocently approached them? They appeared naked and therefore were considered to be completely lacking in morals. Were the pale churchmen ignorant of the fact that their naked state was necessary for survival because women had to fish that way, without clothes, diving from the canoes? The missionaries wanted them to leave their children in their care in order to eradicate the traditions of their ancestors. Didn't they know that their parents, their grandparents, and their great grandparents had handed down a long spiritual tradition of secret ceremonies and wisdom that the young received from the old ones? Finally, didn't they realize how senseless the idea of ownership was to them, useless for the survival of the Yámanas among whom everything is held in common? And, in consequence, how absurd was the white man's overriding obsession, the idea of theft? What meaning could this word have, for which they had been punished and killed?

For Button what the jury called "the massacre" was the fatal result of a series of events and the point where the hatred held back for decades had finally exploded. The price had been paid.

The side door opened, and Logden came in with Chaplain

Bull. Obviously the Court wished to get it over with as soon as possible.

CHAPLAIN BULL:

"Everything done by this Court will be taken up in the Colonial Office, in London. From Jemmy Button's statement it is apparent that he constantly declared his own unwillingness and the unwillingness of his people to go to Keppel Island. There is no direct proof that Button took part in the terrible tragedy although he did take part in the pillaging. His coming on board the *Nancy* voluntarily proves that it was not a premeditated act. We believe it was an act of vengeance carried out by some unidentified natives who felt insulted by the search of their bags. As for future missionary operations: these should be carried out in the natives' countries among the people. The missionary group must be armed in case of emergency. They should live in a stone house, cultivate gardens, and try to teach the natives English."

Jemmy Button was free. Captain Smyley went to him, said something, and they went out the main door together. Coles had been led away. The jury left the room. Some women noisily started to rearrange the chairs and benches.

Outside, a few men went on discussing the events. Nothing was crystal clear. The matter had ended up being more complicated than had been thought at first. Parker Snow's statement had sowed considerable doubt. Interests in the Islands had been touched upon, which this trial would not resolve. And last of all, what proof was there against Button? He had buried the dead, he had come to testify of his own free will. There seemed to be no real charges against him, except the word of a crazy fellow. Coles the cook had not been convincing and did not inspire trust. He was a poor ignorant devil, capable of dozing off during a trial. London spewed hundreds like him into the ships. On the other hand, although Button was a savage, he had a certain prestige. In London he had been famous: hadn't the King received him? Hadn't the newspapers talked about him? And although this had occurred decades before, he still possessed the indefinable aura which even now managed to inspire respect in the whites who approached him.

The icy air opened my lungs. On the grey beach a flock of seagulls quarrelled with the cormorants over the evening meal. The trial had lasted eight hours.

At his lodgings, Smyley was getting his things ready. Despard had given him instructions to return to Tierra del Fuego immediately, recover the schooner *Allen Gardiner*, and return Button to Wulaia. The latter was to point out where the bodies of the missionaries were buried so that the captain might give them a Christian burial. They were to weigh anchor in a couple of hours, as soon as they completed their preparations. As for myself, I had reserved my passage on a ship leaving for Montevideo that very evening.

There was still some light in the heavens, and I had something to do.


Nightfall in the Islands could not be sadder. I walked down to the pier. Near a shack, I saw him. Alone, sitting on a coil of mooring ropes.

I lit my pipe to give myself time and I approached slowly. He crouched when he heard me, as if instinctively looking for stones. When he recognized me, he stood up.

"Jack," his voice was thick, barely audible.

I was not an Englishman. I knew that for him I had never been an Englishman, though English was the only language in which we had been able to communicate.

"Omoy-lume." I gave him a long handshake.

We stood looking at each other for a little while. He

touched his chest and pointed to the *Nancy* to let me know that he would be shipping out. With a quick precise gesture he pointed to the south. It was a hard firm gesture.

He glanced at me again and said:

"Family, sons, well?"

"Very well," I lied.

"How many children and how many wives?" He wanted to know.

I made a vague gesture. He smiled:

"Omoy-lume four wives, nine children, small ones and big ones."

The wind ruffled Jemmy's coarse hair even more. I noticed the wrinkles and fatigue accumulated around his eyes; no doubt he saw the same in mine. Even more wrinkles and fatigue than on the evening of our encounter in the fog.

About fifty metres away, the door of the shack on the wharf opened, and several men dragged out bundles which they loaded into one of the *Nancy's* boats. Against the leaden grey sky of dusk, one of the ships lit its stern lanterns.

"I saw Jack in the big wigwam."

"I had to be there. I came to see you."

He was silent a moment. Then he said in a tired voice:

"The whites ran away howling. But before that we, women and children howled, and nobody listened. Seals and sea lions howled. They left nothing. So we killed. My son also killed. They must not come back," Button was speaking with his eyes fixed on mine, making certain he was delivering a message that must be well understood and passed on. He was searching for words he lacked. He took his time. He wanted everything to be said with the greatest exactitude.

"I understand, Omoy-lume."

Questions made no sense now. He repeated another way what he had already said:

"Deaths no good, Jack; they necessary. Bad times."

"I understand."

Our passage to England was lost for Button in the mist

of time. What had happened there belonged to the memory of others or had been forgotten. Only sometimes would flashes of places and persons and inexplicable things come back. There was madness in the world of the whites, a violence that was not the same violence as hurling stones with a sling or harpooning a big fish.

A man shouted that the boat was ready.

"Goodbye, Jack," Button put out his two hands and gripped my forearms. "Last goodbye."

I grasped his forearms hard:

"We shall not meet again."

"Last time, Jack. No more dreams."

"Goodbye, Omoy-lume."

He climbed nimbly into the boat. The men rowed in a leisurely way. They disappeared behind the hull, then boarded on the port side. A sudden gust of cold wind made me shudder and shook the sails of the ships. I saw Jemmy reappear at the ship's rail. He watched me from there, leaning on his elbows at the stern, alone. With the familiar sound of chains and repeated shouts, the *Nancy* weighed anchor, the sails were unfurled, and the ship began to describe a slow semicircle.

Button remained motionless at the stern, looking in my direction. When the ship turned its prow south, he suddenly removed his shirt and his trousers and flung them into the air, over the side. The small patches fluttered for a second in the air against the sky and fell into the water.

Naked, he raised his arm and held it high; his hand, above, separated its fingers.

I raised my arm.

Having recovered his essential naked state, Button was returning to the profound dream of Tierra del Fuego, to the polar wind, to the freedom of its forests, to the oldest winter in the world, to the tall bonfires in the southern night, to his homeland.

There would be no "subsequent destiny" for the "ill-starred native." Nor for his people nor for anyone in his native land because, by a twist of fate, they would succumb. His own fate and that of his people were sealed. Now the devil existed in Omoy-lume's country.

I am growing old, Mr. MacDowell or MacDowness. There on the wharf, seeing the *Nancy* move away, I felt for the first time that I was growing old. So many cities, taverns, beggars, whores, storms, so many stars seen. The ocean at the world's end, a city like an ocean, Isabella, an albatross with its wings outspread in the wind, the *Encounter* and the *Beagle*, a Yámana woman and her son naked in the falling snow, a sail stiff with ice, two windswept graves, Tasmania and Japan and the Robinson fable with which Mallory taught me how to read, all spin dizzily—like the crazy burden of a maelstrom in my memory—around the infinitely small dot that I am, standing on the wharf in Stanley, watching the *Nancy's* stern tamely disappear into the darkness, heading south.

We are in April and the certainty of autumn is like a balm for the plain exhausted by the summer. I feel like someone convalescing, cautiously testing to see if he can walk. It has been weeks since I finished my story. Since then, lying in bed, I have watched indifferently the passing of the days and nights. Ajax approaches, looks at me the way dogs do and lies down again. Today I finally got ready to put in a few last words and date the sections of this written account to give them some kind of order. It's nothing more than a formality. I've reached the age my father was when he made his final decision. I understand that there are always two roads and then two more, and so on ad infinitum, but in the beginning, only two.

Graciana looks at me as if she recognizes me, happy because I'm getting up to resume an activity now familiar to her. As if something were beginning anew.

Tomorrow, or perhaps this evening if I can find the will to do it, I am going to clear the table, set the oil lamp in the centre, and show her how to hold the pen, dip it into ink, and trace and learn the enigmatic symbols she has patiently watched me living with for so many months. If this is a story for no one, perhaps I should create a reader for it, and perhaps it is she, Mr. MacDowell or MacDowness, who will some day be able to make sense of these papers addressed to no one.

# The Sor Juana Inés de la Cruz Literature Prize

In 1993 the Guadalajara International Book Fair (FIL), the Guadalajara School of Writers (SOGEM) and the French publisher Indigo/Coté-Femmes inaugurated the Sor Juana Inés de la Cruz Prize to recognize the published work of women writers. The award was named after Sor Juana since she was the first female writer of Spanish America, and her poetry, theater and journals constitute an important contribution to the literary arts the world over.

The primary objective of the prize is to bring attention to the work of a female writer in the Spanish language; all female writers who have published a novel in the previous three years are eligible.

The prize includes publication and distribution, under a standard book contract, of the winning entry in Mexico by Fondo de Cultura Económica Press and, since 1995, translation and publication in the United States by Curbstone Press. A presentation of the award is held during the Guadalajara International Book Fair, at which time the winner is presented with a commemorative bronze sculpture of Sor Juana designed by the Portuguese sculptor Gil Simoes.

The winner is selected in the following manner: January, guidelines are made available to the general public; May, deadline for receiving submissions; October, decision of the judges is made public; December, award's ceremony takes place during the Guadalajara International Book Fair. Contact: SOGEM, Av. Circ. Augustín Yáñez #2839, Guadalajara, 44110, JAL, Mexico.

The prize is sponsored by Tequila Sauza S.A. de C.V.; Curbstone Press; Mayor's Office of Zapopan; The Western Technological Institute for Higher Learning, Jalisco; and General Outreach Studies, University of Guadalajara.

# Sor Juana Prize Winners from Curbstone

ASSAULT ON PARADISE
a novel by Tatiana Lobo, translated by Asa Zatz
$15.95pa.   ISBN 1-880684-46-2   320pp

This fast-paced, adventure depicts how the conquistadores and the Church impoverished one world to enrich another.

"On the one hand a hilarious swashbuckling adventure, on the other a bloody, bitter indictment of the Catholic Church in the colonizing of Central America."—*Library Journal*

"...filled with bawdy humor and wryly comic moments, *Assault on Paradise* offers a withering portrait of the Inquisition and the Spanish conquest of the New World."—Jay Parini, *New York Times Book Review*

FIRST LOVE & LOOK FOR MY OBITUARY
Two Novellas by Elena Garro, translated by David Unger
$11.95pa   1-880684-51-9   112pp

"This small book stands out in the landscape of contemporary Mexican fiction."—Donley Watt, *Dallas Morning News*

"This talented Mexican writer transcends geographical barriers and chronology in her depiction of universal emotions and metaphysical problems."—J. Walker, *Choice*

THE LOVE YOU PROMISED ME
a novel by Silvia Molina, translated by David Unger
$14.95pa   1-880684-62-4   208pp

"This lovely work, astonishing in its quietude, was deservedly winner of the Sor Juana Inés de la Cruz Prize and belongs in all literary collections."—*Library Journal*

"For aficionados of Latino literature, this entertaining novel reveals how lovers in modern-day Mexico—as do their US counterparts—face (and fight) familial and societal odds to realize a dream."—*Saludos Hispanos*